The Observer's Book of
ARCHITECTURE

WRITTEN AND ILLUSTRATED BY
JOHN PENOYRE, R.I.B.A.

AND

MICHAEL RYAN, R.I.B.A.

FOREWORD BY
F. R. S. YORKE, F.R.I.B.A.

D1481520

FREDERICK WARNE & CO LTD
FREDERICK WARNE & CO INC
LONDON: NEW YORK

FOREWORD

Architecture in any age is conditioned by the contemporary system of economy, methods of production, and requirements of society; but it has its roots in the past. This is not to say that any great architecture is a reproduction of the work of an earlier period, but that the sense of scale and proportion and the handling of the texture and colour of building materials are not invented afresh by every generation. They come partly from the inspiration we get from new demands and the new methods we have for meeting them, and partly from the rich legacy of building tradition.

It is important, if we are to get a full enjoyment from observing the architecture of this or any former time, that we should know something of the conditions on which the style is founded.

In this stimulating and extraordinarily well-balanced book Penoyre and Ryan have traced quite clearly—so clearly that I found it possible to understand the text without the diagrams—the development of English architecture from Saxon times, and have provided just the background that the observer needs to help him follow, without confusion or bogging down in unnecessary detail, the development of building, planning, and technique through the centuries; and that should help, too, to get rid of some of the misgivings he may have about the architecture of today.

F. R. S. Y.

*

Third edition (revised and reset)
© Frederick Warne & Co., Ltd.
London, England, 1975

LIBRARY OF CONGRESS CATALOG CARD NO. 74–80610
ISBN 0 7232 1537 5

Printed in Great Britain by
William Clowes & Sons, Limited
London, Beccles and Colchester
132.1174

CONTENTS

*

		PAGE
Foreword		4
Introduction		6

Part One **Buildings of the Medieval Period**

1	Pre-Conquest or Saxon	20
2	Norman or Romanesque	25
3	The Early English Period	39
4	The Decorated Period	51
5	The Perpendicular Period	60

Part Two **Buildings of the Transitional Period**

6	Renaissance	73
7	Tudor	80
8	Elizabethan and Jacobean	89

Part Three **Buildings of the Classical Era**

| 9 | Inigo Jones and Christopher Wren | 99 |
| 10 | The Eighteenth Century | 109 |

Part Four **Buildings of the Industrial Era**

| 11 | The Nineteenth Century | 119 |
| 12 | The Twentieth Century | 129 |

Visual Index

Character, 140 Columns, 160 Vaults
and ceilings, 166 Doorways, 173
Windows, 181

Endpapers
Front: Map showing the distribution of
Traditional Building Materials of Great
Britain *Back:* Illustrated Glossary of
Classical and Renaissance Terms

INTRODUCTION

*

Architecture implies building beautifully and well. Great architecture can be profoundly moving, can stir us more deeply than any other of the visual arts, for it is a three-dimensional art into which the beholder may enter and of which he may feel himself to be an integral part. Architecture is not the application of beautiful detail to a building; to aspire to the name of architecture the building itself must not only be well built but must truly fulfil its purpose and at the same time delight the beholder.

But what is architecture? Is it every structure made and built by man for his use and shelter, or is it solely the great and famous buildings erected as temples, palaces or seats of government? What distinguishes a work of architecture from one of mere technology?

Architecture is an art and art lifts the spirit and excites the emotions to wonder, awe or joy. But architecture cannot exist without a sound technology. We cannot define art, but we believe that the principles outlined in this book will help to clarify for each reader his own interpretation of architecture, what it is and how it appeals to him. Perhaps as well it may help him to put into perspective the architectural problems and achievements of today.

Architecture is a synthesis of art and technology, reflecting in outward form the wealth or poverty of the builders, the pattern of their lives, their hopes and ideas and their social development. This is true of cottages and castles, of great works of engineering, of churches and cathedrals and of the houses of ordinary people, for who is to say

6

that the dedication, care and love lavished on the humbler or more utilitarian structures do not often enough shine through these works and establish them as art as surely as the intellects of the famous men who designed our cathedrals and palaces assure their works a place in the lists of fame?

The factors that govern the form of any building are three—its purpose, or the needs of the builders; the skill of the builders themselves, in which we include their knowledge and traditions; and the materials that are most readily available. Since social needs and technical skill both change in time with the history of the country, and since it is to the progressive change of social condition that architecture owes its changing form in different ages, this review is treated chronologically.

Primarily, this is a reference book, designed specifically to give the observer the information he wants in a form easily remembered. Buildings of various periods look as they do for very definite reasons, and these reasons are explained as far as possible in the text; but their actual appearance and basic characteristics are less easily explained in words. They must be illustrated, even caricatured, if their qualities are to be fully appreciated.

Hence the majority of the illustrations in the book are not exact representations of particular buildings; they are generalizations of essentials.

At the end of the book will be found an index—again wholly illustrative in character—which has been called the Visual Index. Its purpose is to group together certain features (doors, columns, etc.) in such a way that the observer, when faced with a building for identification, may note for himself its peculiar elements, compare them to their equivalents or approximate equivalents in the Visual Index, and then refer to the text as indicated.

In the first section of the Index, Architectural Character, an attempt has been made to illustrate the atmosphere and the 'feeling' of the various periods without reference to particular details, as it is found that general character is often of paramount importance in the identification of periods.

The Index, however, must be used with some caution, for the presence of details that belong to a specific period by no means ensures that the building in which they occur actually belongs to that period. In the 19th century many buildings were erected as virtual replicas of those of previous ages. They are often very beautiful and scholarly reproductions, and here, if they are to be distinguished from buildings of the periods they imitate, such factors as apparent age and the inherent probability of such a building existing at that place and time must be taken into account. It has been said that for enjoyment of architecture a knowledge of dates is unimportant, and if pure aesthetic appreciation were the only benefit to be derived from a study of architecture this would be true. Archaeological interest, historical association, an understanding of the aesthetic climate of the time and of structural problems and how they were overcome, all contribute to our enjoyment. Without some knowledge of dates this enjoyment would all be missed.

English architecture is an immense subject for so small a work, and in order to cover the ground it has been necessary to generalize, possibly at the expense of strict accuracy in some particulars. But the main story is clear and it is a story well worth learning, for in England there exists more beautiful architecture than in almost any country in the world.

Building Materials (see map on endpaper)

The subject of building materials is susceptible to no such chronological treatment as the other factors we have mentioned, for whereas skill and social needs change as time passes, and are more or less the same in all parts of the country at any one time, the materials available vary with locality, and change hardly at all with the passage of time. So some account of building materials, their uses and localities, must be given before coming to the main building story. Having once described these, no further specific reference will be made to local variations due to their influence.

In the days of bad communications, when a journey from London to Gloucester took three days if travelling light or nearly a week for heavy transport in good weather, clearly only the most expensive and elaborate buildings could afford to use any but local materials, and even then seldom for the main structure. Thus until the 18th and 19th centuries and the digging of canals and the laying of railways, local materials were all-important to local buildings. After this time cheap water transport inland, cheap coastwise traffic, and cheap railways enabled houses to be built often more economically in brick than in the local material. Churches and castles are the great exceptions to the general rule. The importance of religion and war to the medieval peoples was such that, if humanly possible, stone, the

9

noblest and most lasting of their materials, would be transported for the work. Here water transport was used. The stone was quarried at a suitable coastal quarry and brought by ship round the coast and up the rivers until it could be shipped no further. After this it had to be carried overland by packhorse.

The first and the most primitive building material is timber. Oak is the traditional English timber, all other woods that are useful structurally being foreigners, with the exception of elm, which is most usefully employed in connection with water, as in jetties, water-pipes, or as the outer sheathing to a building, like weather-boarding. At one time England was a densely forested land, the greater parts of the low-lying districts being covered with oak woods. The 17th century saw the end of timber as the material for large houses. After this, timber had become too scarce owing to the inroads made in the forests by the charcoal burners and the farmers.

Subsequently only the smallest cottages in remote districts were built of oak. Later, in the 18th century, foreign softwood became available, especially in coastal areas of the south-east, and a temporary return to timber weather-boarding in sawn deal may be seen in districts that had a strong timber tradition. The principal districts for timber buildings are the Western Midlands (notably Worcestershire, Shropshire, Cheshire, and Lancashire), East Anglia, and Kent.

Building stones vary greatly from the hard granite of the west and north to the flints and chalk of East Anglia. But the best stone lies between these two extremes. This is the limestone that runs in a great belt across the country from Dorset through east Somerset, Gloucestershire, north Wiltshire, Oxfordshire, Northampton, Leicestershire, Nottinghamshire, to east Yorkshire. This limestone is one of the finest building stones in the world, and all along its track masons have taken advantage of its good weathering qualities, its ease of working, and its consistent texture, and a splendid building tradition has grown up wherever it occurs. This is perhaps most noticeable of all in the Cotswolds. Sandstones occur in the Midlands and in Yorkshire, but they are either hard and difficult to work or else they have comparatively poor weathering qualities and strength and are too friable. Chalk from the hard lower strata was used for building stone, although very rarely in this century. But chalk may be burnt for lime to make plaster, and in chalk there lie strata of flints. Brick and flint or stone and flint and much thick plasterwork may be expected in the chalk districts, the principal areas being east Dorset, Hampshire and Wiltshire, Salisbury Plain, the North and South Downs, and Kent, the Berkshire Downs, the Chilterns, Suffolk and Norfolk, and a small part of east Yorkshire. The hard rocks of the north and west, the millstone grit of the Pennines, and the granites of Wales and Cornwall are not easily worked and are very strong. Buildings in these areas tend to be very simple and rather crude.

The clay of the valley bottoms has since the time of the Romans been used for making bricks, but this material was not generally used until the 16th century, when timber was becoming scarce. Generally speaking, oak forests grow best on a clay subsoil, so from early times a combination of brick and timber was common, and later brick alone may be expected in most clay districts. East Anglia was the home of brick-making in medieval times, and still today more bricks are made in south-east England than anywhere else in the British Isles.

Social Conditions

Before starting a more detailed review of the Architecture of England, it is necessary to relate, in a very general way, the sequence of changing social conditions and the predominating building types that arose because of these conditions.

Broadly speaking, there are three main periods into which English architecture may be split: the Medieval, the Renaissance, and the Industrial.

The first, Medieval, covers a period during which men were influenced as never since by a tremendous religious preoccupation and fervour, and when life was very insecure.

The second, Renaissance, covers a period when intellect was considered all-important, religion had gone through all the changes of emphasis implied by the Reformation, and social organization had advanced to a stage where a reasonable degree of security was assured.

The third, Industrial, period was that during which men were building for gain, when religion played an even smaller part in men's lives; and when England, after the defeat of Napoleon in the most expensive war she had fought, enjoyed a whole century of almost complete peace and a great measure of security for the individual.

Between these periods there came times of transition. One period slid either more or less rapidly into the next, the influences of the one greatly affecting the other, so that hard-and-fast boundaries of 'period' become meaningless.

The Medieval period, which extended from the Dark Ages to the Reformation (about A.D. 600 to 1500), was far the longest of the three. During the whole of this time the buildings on which men lavished their greatest skill and care were those of a religious nature. The remainder are nearly all castles, which were built to subdue the country after the conquest, to house the feudal lords, and to form part of a chain of defensive strong-points throughout the land. Castles continued to be built on a more and more elaborate scale until the end of the 15th century, when the use of gun-powder had made them an anachronism, and the country was sufficiently secure internally to allow men to live without a constant fear that their neighbours might attack them.

At the beginning of this period, when the Saxons were newly converted to Christianity, the people were living a life of little security, and had very little skill in building in anything but timber. Their buildings have now nearly all disappeared except the crude stone churches, small and ill-lit, reflecting vividly the difficulties they had in overcoming the problems of what was to them an unusual building material. The constant invasions and threats of invasions gave them little inclination to undertake any very large-scale works and so they learnt better ways of building extremely slowly. Although association with the Continent seems to have been fairly constant, they hardly benefited at all by the much greater skill of the Latin peoples.

When the Normans occupied the land they brought their superior technical skill with them, and taught the Saxon how to build in the Norman manner. But since they had to use Saxon labour, semi-skilled by their standards, their buildings were at first very rough in finish, and their walls were built a good deal thicker than they need have been had they been able to cut their stones more accurately. As time passed building technique became more perfect, until by the end of the 15th century a pitch of technical ability in masonry and carpentry was reached in England that has never been surpassed. All this time the great majority of buildings, that is the ordinary houses of the people, were in timber. What they were like in the early days we can only guess, for none have survived, but they were probably for the most part closely built clusters of single-storey, timber-framed houses, walled with woven osiers plastered with mud, and roofed with thatch. These houses were built under the shadow of the castles or huddled together inside their curtain walls for protection.

Later, with the increase of population, prosperity and trade, proper cities were formed. Most of the buildings were still in timber, except for the castles, churches, and monasteries, but there began to be formed a middle-class, not rich enough to build castles yet not the unpaid servant class. These people built themselves farms and, when well-to-do, manor-houses. These were often of stone or brick.

The vast majority of buildings in this period then are ecclesiastical, with a number of castles that later give place to manor-houses. Although there are certain other sorts of buildings besides, these are the main types that dominate the Medieval era.

By Tudor times enough churches and cathedrals

had been built to meet the needs of the people, and the final break between the Church and the Crown, always an uneasy team, resulted not only in the destruction of many monasteries but in an almost complete cessation of ecclesiastical building in favour of secular. Men now, during the Tudor age, had a greatly increased idea of material comforts. The wealth of the country was more evenly distributed than before and many country squires could afford to build themselves strong brick or oak houses. Cheap bricks had become universally popular. Even the king considered that the material was suitable for his palaces. Gone was the time when only the greatest in the land could build in enduring stone, while the remainder built in mud and thatch; gone was the great church-building era. Domestic building in lasting materials had become possible for all but the poorest.

This, the beginning of the Renaissance in England, was a period of great mental and social upheavals. Not only was the omnipotence of Rome called in question and finally renounced in favour of new religious beliefs, but a deeper change which made such renunciation possible had come over the mentality of the people. This was a change from an unquestioning acceptance of the established order of social life and an un-questioning faith in the teachings of the Church, to an enquiring, experimenting attitude of mind that was a most adventurous departure from the well-known safe channels to which thought had hitherto been confined. This spirit of adventure encouraged enquiry on a rational and material basis, totally opposed to all previous beliefs. It is the spirit of reason which was the mainspring of all activities for the next two hundred years.

Under these circumstances material comforts and improvements in domestic building were natural, and the 17th and 18th centuries show a complete revolution in domestic architecture followed by a full development of the ordinary middle-class person's house, from the small medieval manor-house to the elegant, comfortable residence of the Georgian gentleman, a process greatly helped by the rapidly increasing wealth of the country.

One important and immediate result of the Renaissance was that learning was made possible for anyone who cared to acquire it, and was no longer confined to the monks and friars. A great number of colleges and schools were consequently founded in the Tudor period, and this class of building continued to be of some importance during succeeding centuries.

By the 18th century the social order had again acquired a stability that seemed as permanent as the old feudal system. Wealth was concentrated once more into fewer hands and vast country estates were enclosed by wealthy men, to the exclusion of the small farmer. On these estates were built immense country homes of unparalleled grandeur. In the towns whole neighbourhoods were owned by single landowners, who were thus able to lay them out as residential building estates, making possible an organized town-planning of fine blocks of houses arranged in stately squares and crescents, a circumstance that would not have been possible had each inhabitant built and planned his own home as he had done in medieval times.

On the other hand land enclosure in the country and increased industrial activity in the coal and iron producing centres had resulted in the formation of new towns, towards which the dispossessed small-holder was inevitably drawn. During the 18th and 19th centuries, a prodigious increase in population took place; the reason for this is not certainly known. New homes had to be built for these people, and new factories sprang up everywhere, with their attendant interminable rows of depressing, cheap houses.

The last ten years of the 18th century and the first seventy-five of the 19th constitute a period of industrial development that proceeded at an almost frightening pace. This was made possible by the fact that coal and iron were available together in many parts of the country.

The industrial era cannot be said to have started at any particular date. Long ago in Tudor times machinery was in use for performing many of the processes in the manufacture of woollen cloth; and for the simpler tasks, such as grinding corn, machinery had been in existence for centuries before that. At first this was wooden machinery driven by water-power or wind-power. By this arrangement the workpeople were distributed over the length of the rivers that supplied the power, and not concentrated in towns. In 1712 a stationary steam-engine was invented and put to work pumping water from the mines in Cornwall. This machine was made partly of wood and was very simple and ponderous, but it marked a most important milestone in the development of the industrial revolution. The production of iron in bulk could not be achieved until a method was devised of using coal for smelting, for the universal fuel, wood, was fast disappearing. Late in the 18th century this difficulty was overcome, and iron became available in ever-increasing quantities to make machines for pumping out the new deep coal-mines and for working the manufactories, to make bridges, railways, and finally, ships. From 1790 onwards the output of manufactured goods from the factories doubled and trebled every few years. The increase in goods traffic was enormous. At first elaborate canal systems were built; then railways were laid down. The first steam locomotive was in operation in 1804, a hundred years after the first steam-engine was used, and the first public railway was opened in 1825. Great engineering works in connection with transport were undertaken. Iron bridges, iron railway stations, tremendous tunnels, cuttings, and embankments, 'vaster', as Ruskin says, 'than the walls of Babylon'—all were executed at a great pace.

Meanwhile the workpeople of the towns, whence all the flood of manufactured articles originated, were increasing and multiplying at a rate that exceeded the employment demand. Consequently labour was cheap, housing was bad, slums appalling and profits vast.

Business increased with manufacture, so huge office blocks and banking-houses were needed, and the increased urban population made the invention of blocks of tenements and flats a necessity. Large shops and warehouses were built to deal with the ever-increasing flow of customers and goods; compulsory education was introduced and thousands of schools built; hospitals and public buildings of every sort were needed for the new towns and much 'municipal' building was done.

The increasing efficiency of passenger transport

gradually allowed more and more people to live outside the towns, and as the prosperity of the country grew, so gradually the standard of living, which had dropped swiftly because of the increase in population, improved. In the late 19th and early 20th centuries these factors showed themselves in the growth of the suburban house. Although these small houses were a vast improvement on the crowded slums they helped to replace, they were mostly badly built, and since no organization existed for town-planning they were almost invariably built in the wrong place. The necessity for a controlled planning of building activities on a national basis became more and more obvious as time passed, and gradually the old laws of property-ownership were modified to allow a greater measure of control to be exercised over the building activities of individuals. Now sufficient powers have been given to the authorities to permit a really efficient planning scheme that applies to both country and town to be realized.

During the 19th century the principal types of buildings were industrial, commercial, and civic. In the 20th century the accent has been on domestic building and the improvement of public services, for today the demand is primarily for a higher standard of public health and education and for a more congenial environment for people to live in. Up to the end of the 18th century an ordered existence in England was possible. In the 19th century life became chaotic, for the increase in the speed of developments was much too sudden. It is the rectifying of the state of affairs which the industrial revolution brought about that is the chief concern of architects and planners today.

*

PART ONE

BUILDINGS OF THE MEDIEVAL PERIOD

*

CHAPTER 1

Pre-Conquest or Saxon
THE DARK AGES

*

Saxon churches are the oldest English buildings. We are not concerned here with the buildings of the Romans, visitors from abroad, nor with the mysterious works of the prehistoric peoples, but with a more homely subject—the parish church.

'Saxon' is a convenient name for all English buildings of the Dark Ages, regardless of who actually built them.

There are very few complete Saxon churches left, but these show clearly of what the inhabitants of England were capable in this era.

Compared to the peoples of later centuries the Saxons were a primitive and uneducated folk, but in the very earliest part of this period, during the time of the Venerable Bede, there existed in the religious establishments in England greater minds and a higher culture than anything on the continent of Europe. But this was not to last. Heathen invasions from across the North Sea and internal wars played havoc with any possible progress, and the whole period is characterized by a series of more or less partial lapses into heathenism. During one of the longer periods of comparative stability, the country having become once again largely Christian, a considerable amount of church building was undertaken. It is from this period (600–800) that most Saxon churches probably date. Later, more heathens— Danes—invaded the country and destroyed many churches, and during the whole period of 800– 1000 very little building appears to have been undertaken. It is not till the Norman conquest, or shortly before, that any real progress can be seen in building technique.

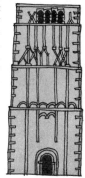

Saxon Tower

Of the few Saxon churches that remain, and churches are almost the only buildings that have lasted, all are small. They are the simplest possible sort of building. The Saxons evidently had no idea of thinking of a church as anything more than a series of rooms joined together by narrow doorways. They built up their churches piecemeal like children playing with bricks. That the chancel and nave should be thought of as part of the same enclosed space had not occurrred to them. They made the chancel arch so small and heavy that, whilst emphasizing the shrine-like quality of the chancel, they completely cut it off from the body of the church.

Although complete Saxon buildings are very rare, many churches have

PORCH CHANCEL

NAVE

21

Saxon work in them, and there are a number of smaller works such as stone crosses erected to mark the old crossings of ways. The Saxons were great tower-builders and it is this, the strongest part of the church, that has most often survived. Later enlargements of the structure have in many cases been made so long ago that it is often only by the details of the masonry that the earlier work may be distinguished. The exteriors of the churches were simple and were sometimes decorated with a criss-cross pattern, formed of long, thin  stones let into the face of the rubble wall, that seems to have little meaning or purpose. This decoration may be a derivation of Roman building forms, so debased as to be unrecognizable; or it may be derived from timber construction with which the Saxons were very familiar. The use of alternate vertical and horizontal stones at the corners, which is a debased form of the logical pattern made by any stone-mason who wants to make a strong corner to his building, is very typical of

Normal (L) and Saxon (R) corner stones

22

the awkward way in which the Saxons used stone, for timber was their natural traditional material, originating as they did from the forests of Northern Germany and Denmark.

Their windows and doors are like very small holes punched in very thick walls. Their windows are usually placed singly with round arches over them, or sometimes with only a simple triangle of stones instead of an arch. Where they ventured

to make larger openings they used short pillars to support the walls above. These were either plain shafts of stone or were crudely carved like balusters.

No roofs exist, for they have all long since disappeared, but there is a roof of a Saxon tower at Sompting, in Sussex, which is almost certainly original in shape.

The hall-mark of Saxon work is its crudeness and smallness; when looking at Saxon work one feels more strongly than with that of any other period how remote and primitive the builders were.

CHAPTER 2

Norman or Romanesque

11TH AND 12TH CENTURIES

*

Norman building has become a synonym for solidity. What more rock-like and enduring than the Norman castle keep? What more massive than the vast cylinders of dressed stone that support the Norman church?

This was a new way of building, more ambitious and greater in size and scope than anything the primitive Saxons had been able to achieve.

Some big building in the French manner, however, had been undertaken before the actual landings by the Normans under William of Normandy in 1066, for communications with the Continent had greatly improved. A much earlier Westminster Abbey than the existing structure was built before the Conquest, and a fine work it must have been.

England was at last progressing, and she was ripe for new ideas.

After his decisive defeat of Harold at Hastings, Duke William set about subduing and organizing the country in the most businesslike manner. He brought with him his court, his lords, and his barons. He brought his highly organized and zealous churchmen, and he brought his soldiers, his common people. The social system that existed in England was as well suited to a military as it was to a more peaceful way of life, and he modified it but little. Under this system the

HEREFORD CATHEDRAL: EARLY 12th CENTURY

unpaid serf gave his work and his service to his master in return for the protection and security that his master's organized household could afford him; the household organized for defence and for agriculture.   The freed man who was in a position to employ unpaid serfs would receive his land from his next social superior, and would pay rent to him in the form of men-at-arms on demand in case of need.   The small barons rented their land from the great barons on the same basis, and they in their turn were granted manors, or large tracts of land, from the king, who would demand a very considerable payment for his grant.   This, the feudal system, was ideal for a population made up of isolated communities, organized on a military basis, and all owing allegiance to one king.

William's first task was to make the country secure, and to do this he granted his barons permission to build castles on their manors, strongholds to overawe the Saxons by their magnitude and to serve as strongpoints in case of rebellion. As a temporary measure the barons built themselves wooden castles, later replacing them by

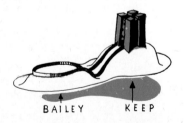

Norman Castle

huge stone keeps which they used not only to maintain order within their own domains and to house themselves and their garrison, but also as bases from which to harass the neighbouring barons, in order to secure more land for themselves.

The second of William's great tasks was to establish his church. He and his people were ardent Christians, and after the initial period of warfare had ceased, during which no church building took place, a very great number of

Norman Church

parish churches, cathedrals, abbeys and monasteries was built. The cathedrals were to be the largest buildings ever seen in this country, buildings that must have amazed the Saxons who, of course, had to do most of the work.

Thus, early in the Norman period social and therefore building activities split naturally into two divisions—secular and religious. Secular buildings, after the initial castle-building era, became relatively unimportant. Religious buildings continued to gain in importance and size until the Reformation.

The main characteristic of all Norman work is its massiveness and its roundness: round arches, massive cylindrical columns, thick flat walls, and sometimes round buildings altogether like the Temple Church in London or the chapel at Ludlow Castle. To the Norman designer the square and the circle were the most important shapes. The Normans built with small stones, and using, as they did, partially skilled Saxon labour, their early walls and pillars were very

27

crudely built. Their method was to rely on the dead weight and solidity of their walls to take the sideways thrust of the arches. They used only a few shallow buttresses, mere thickenings of the walls, to take the added loads at special points. They cut as few stones as they could, making their walls and pillars of two skins of cut stones and filling in the space inside with rubble. This method is not so strong as building with larger and properly fitted stones, so they had to make their walls and piers much thicker than they would otherwise have needed to do, which in its turn increased the weight that had to be supported—a vicious circle. Small wonder that their pillars look so thick and massive.

This method was most unsatisfactory and cases are known where a whole tower fell down almost as soon as it was built. This happened at Winchester Cathedral.

These towers were squat and square, lending to all Norman churches and cathedrals a stocky appearance that is unmistakable. In the bigger

28

churches and cathedrals the pillars, thick and round, supported semi-circular arches to hold the

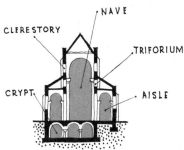

high walls of the clerestory above. The space made by the aisle roofs was sometimes used for another small arcade of arches, the triforium, which made a passage-way round the building at a high level and helped to lighten the heavy wall.

Perhaps the most interesting feature of Norman buildings is the roof. Usually they roofed their buildings with timber, boarding in the roof-trusses to make a tunnel-shaped ceiling, but from the earliest stages they put stone vaulted roofs to their underground crypts, where it was easy to construct in the heavier material at ground level. Later, they made stone roofs for the main parts of the building too, partly because they wanted their important buildings to be as durable as possible, for the risk of fire to a wooden roof was very real. But roofs were not altogether of stone. They built a stone inner vault and put a steep wooden roof on top of it.

The development of the stone inner vault is so important that it is given here in detail. Not only is it intrinsically interesting but it illustrates most aptly that structural necessity and practical requirements were the cause of the introduction of features in a building that give it its 'style', and that style was by no means a pleasing way of building which the builders used because they

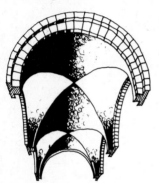

thought it 'looked nice'. At the same time a preconceived idea of what a building should be, before ways and means of making it so are discussed, is bound to influence the general shape of a building. For instance, the powerful but almost unconscious desire for their churches to aspire and to have a sense of mystic magnificence and reaching for the heavens, undoubtedly made the Medieval church-builders want to build as high as they dared and want to make their roofs look as light and delicate as possible. It is from these basic desires that the method of construction largely springs, and from the necessities of the construction that those shapes arise that people so often think of as the hall-marks of a 'style'. The true hall-mark of a period is the shape, the proportion, the method of construction and the details all thought of as a whole, and all arising from the basic idea behind the building. This idea was itself absolutely governed by the lives and thoughts of the people of the time, by their needs and aspirations, by their way of looking at things, and the ratio in which they held some things to be more important than others. It is only by study of the peoples' lives and thoughts that a real understanding of architecture may be derived. However, the scope of this book is not wide enough to allow of any very detailed account of these matters, but because no further stress is laid on this aspect of architecture it is not to be thought that it is unimportant.

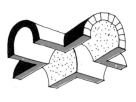

The most elementary sort of vault known to the Normans was the Barrel Vault, which was simply a tunnel; by making two barrel vaults intersect at right-angles, a groined cross-vault was achieved. This was built solidly of thick masonry, requiring a very strong wooden frame to hold the stones in place while it was being built, making a roof to the

square intersection of two equally wide passageways. If, however, a vaulted roof to an arcade of arches is required, it is possible to repeat the central motif alone and omit the 'barrels'. This the Normans did, usually in their crypts.

In order, however, to lessen the amount of tim-

ber centering, as the temporary support is called, they found it convenient to build proper arches between the columns first, and build the groined vault between them afterwards. This was the most usual way of building a groined vault. But the vault was not, even so, very strong. The junction between the two original barrels along the groins was always weak. In attempting to overcome this difficulty and in attempting to make the shape of their roofs more definite and pleasing to the eye, they hit upon the plan of making diagonal arches first, quite separately, as self-supporting members, and filling in between the diagonal and side arches with comparatively thin panels of stone work. This is a much stronger roof and an easier one to make, but as soon as it was tried the question arose of what was the best shape for the diagonal arches to take. As the diagonal ribs were to be semi-circular arches, then the top of the vault would be a great deal higher in the centre than at the sides, producing a series of inverted saucers. This was not a popular solution to the problem in this country, and it was solved at first by making the diagonal a much flatter arch, i.e. segmental, not semi-circular. This looks awkward and does not carry the vertical line of the column smoothly into the roof. Peterborough Cathedral aisles are an example. All these vaults, how- ever, were only suitable for roofing over squares. If the plan demanded an oblong shape, the arches along the long sides became much higher than those along the short sides. 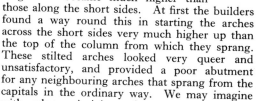 At first the builders found a way round this in starting the arches across the short sides very much higher up than the top of the column from which they sprang. These stilted arches looked very queer and unsatisfactory, and provided a poor abutment for any neighbouring arches that sprang from the capitals in the ordinary way. We may imagine with what misgivings the man who first thought of using a pointed arch tried the experiment. But a poin- ted arch was to be the solu- tion to all the difficulties. Not only could its amount of pointedness be varied without jarring on the eye, allowing unequal spans to be the same height at  the top, but it allowed the big diagonal rib to spring vertically from the capital in a strong true sweep that continued upwards the even flow of the columns and carried the eye straight to the highest point of the building. From this stage vaulting problems were easily over- come. Now it was merely a matter of refine- ment.

The pointed arch was invented and used in Durham Cathedral as early as 1130, but did not come into general use till the end of the century.

Norman windows and doors were small, round-headed openings in thick walls. Often if they wanted a simple rectangular door they filled in the arch with a large, semi-circular stone called a tympanum. This they decorated with spirited

carvings which were of a character that is easily recognized. Lively and often humorous, the Norman carver had a technique that is inimitable. He seldom attempted anything other than low relief and his subjects though ostensibly religious, were, when he carved a scene with people in it, frankly secular in feeling. Simple abstract patterns mixed with stiff, formal foliage were much used, often in early work based on intertwining basket-work designs of Celtic origin. The arches over their windows and doors, more particularly over the latter, often consisted not of one thick

arch but of a series of concentric rings of arches, receding into the thickness of the wall. These were normally carved, each ring of stones with a different pattern, and each stone being carved as one whole section of a repeating motif, irrespective of its size. This gave a slightly irregular quality to their carving which is extremely pleasing to the eye. Some doors have as many as six or seven columns each side, supporting six or seven arches. The capitals of the Norman columns are often elaborately carved with beasts

and stiff formal foliage, but the most usual capital consists of a large flat square stone, or abacus, on which to build the arch spring, and beneath it a deep 'cushion cap' which changes the square shape of the arch spring into the round shape of the column. On very thick columns the typical scalloped pattern that this change of shape suggested was repeated many times, and the abacus was sometimes made in the form of an octagon. In the more highly

35

decorated buildings the shafts of the columns were carved with big zigzags and spirals. The feet of the columns were normally very simply treated, with a wider course of stones at the bottom to spread the weight, carved into a round-shaped moulding, sitting on a square of masonry. Sometimes the corners of the square were covered over with a leaf to make them look more finished.

The Norman staircase that was used in both church and castle was of the ordinary spiral sort with a vertical central shaft, each step being built into the wall at one end and leaving a round lump at the other which became the shaft. This sort of staircase was universal and was the only sort of stone stair in general use in this country for hundreds of years.

All the details and constructional features that apply to churches and cathedrals apply to castles also. But here the main plan was, of course, very different. The principal object of a castle is its durability and its ability to withstand siege-engines, battering-rams, mines, and so on. A high square tower with immensely thick walls and narrow round-headed windows is the essence of the Norman castle. This is the keep, and it stands isolated from the other castle walls. A curtain wall surrounds the keep with a bailey, or open court, between and often round the whole work flows a river, or at least a ditch would be dug.

In times of danger the poor people, the baron's serfs, retainers and cattle, would herd inside the walls for protection. The living-quarters of the baron himself were in the keep, and a cheerless, comfortless place it must have been. No glass in the windows—only oak shutters to temper the icy winds—rushes on the stone floor, and the smoke from the roaring fire escaping where it might through windows and roof, blackening the stone walls and ruining the tapestries that were carefully stitched by the womenfolk to make the place a little less grim, for it was only the most palatial keeps that had the luxurious fireplace, a round-arched recess with a crude flue that led through the outside wall.

It is on this note of uncompromising grimness that we leave the Normans, and we will see how the forthright square-and-circle thinking of this period slides into the more highly developed and sophisticated austerity of the next.

37

CHAPTER 3

The Early English Period
13TH CENTURY

*

This is the earliest phase of Gothic Architecture. Gothic was a derogatory term implying barbarity, given to Medieval architecture by the classicists of the 18th century, a most inappropriate label for the splendid ecclesiastical buildings of the 13th and 14th centuries. The Early English style of building covers the period when England was becoming more settled, when the distinction between Norman and Saxon was becoming less marked, and when the complete autocracy of the sovereign had been destroyed by a community of nobles who must already have felt themselves to be English.

The Crusades of the 12th century had enabled the Normans to learn much of Eastern architecture, particularly of Eastern military engineering, in which the Saracens excelled. Intercourse with the continent of Europe was constant, and new ideas there were immediately adopted at home. It was during this period that the high ideology of the Medieval church became fully developed. Desire for salvation and fear of damnation gave rise to a preoccupation with life after death that had probably not been equalled since the days of Ancient Egypt.

Outside the body of the church few could read or write, so Medieval builders symbolized their religious beliefs in wood and stone, making their churches and cathedrals dramatized representations of their ideals, and incorporating in them

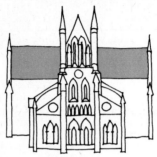

Early English Cathedral

such incidental and picturesque stories from the Bible as could be rendered in carving and stained glass. The Early English builders made their churches as austere as possible, a symbol of the renunciation of the flesh and of worldly riches. They built their cathedrals as high as they dared, a symbol of man reaching to heaven; from such inspiration came the dark, tall cathedrals and the austere and simple parish churches of the 13th century.

Early English Parish Church

The huge endowments of the monasteries enabled ecclesiastical buildings to be undertaken on an ever-increasing scale. The Church at this time owned as much as a fifth of the land, and the importance of the monastic establishments can hardly be over-emphasized. Quite apart from being the centres that fostered the all-pervading influence of religious thought, the monasteries had almost the entire monopoly of learning. Such knowledge of medicine as existed, the most up-to-date theories of agriculture and, above all, the science of architecture were, if not the exclusive property of the monasteries, certainly fostered directly by them.

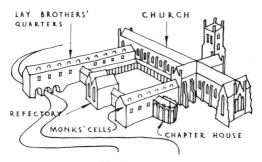

The Monastery

A large monastery consisted essentially of the monastic church, the cloister, the chapter house, the sacristy and the living quarters of the monks. The living quarters consisted of the dormitory, the refectory and the kitchens. The dormitory frequently adjoined the church and, in the establishments of certain orders, consisted of a series of cells. The chapter house often consisted of a separate building, a polygonal vaulted chamber of great beauty, in which the business of the establishment, both secular and spiritual, was transacted. The dissolution of the monasteries in the time of Henry VIII was so wholesale that none now exist except in a ruined condition. The monastic churches, however, frequently survived, the larger ones often achieving cathedral status.

Engineering skill had greatly increased during the last 50 years, and builders had come to a proper understanding of the thrusts set up inside a structure based on arches. Stone cutting was by now improved out of all recognition, so that although churches were built much taller than before, their supports could become more slender and the whole structure very much lighter. Pillars were now built of solid dressed stones all fitting tightly together and able to bear greatly increased weights, but most walls were still built with rubble cores as before.

The structural principle of the Early English church is that walls are only built thick enough to withstand the sideways pushing of the arches at those points where the arches join them. Between these points the wall may be as thin as practicable. This means that if the roof and vaulting thrusts come between the windows, there the wall is made immensely thick. The thickening of the wall had to be so deep that it became in fact a short cross-wall that took the thrust along its length. The lighting of large churches and cathedrals complicated the problem, for with so wide a building it is necessary to have more light than could be admitted through side windows only, or the centre of the building would remain dark. So the centre of all big churches is raised up and clerestory windows are built in. The thrust of the vault of the main roof, however, has now to be transferred across the aisle roof to the supporting buttresses.

An arch flung across the gap at an angle was found to be a solution. These flying buttresses, which may be compared with the familiar timber shoring seen supporting many buildings when under reconstruction, take the weight of the nave roof and vaulting, and pass it downwards and outwards to the great buttresses on the outer wall. Pinnacles were put on top of the thin buttress walls to give them added weight. Where the flying buttress puts its weight on to the main buttress, so the main buttress is made correspondingly thicker to take the added strain, the thickenings being sloped off to shed the rainwater. In small buildings the buttresses were shallower because the load was less.

43

The builders did not attempt to hide their methods of construction; they did not conceal the flying buttresses, but let their buildings assume the shape dictated by structural necessity. Thirteenth-century exteriors are almost undecorated; simple expressions of engineering in dressed stone.

How much more they are however than the mere outcome of applied technology is a measure of the spirit that inspired their builders. The works of men are inspired by man and in them he expresses, consciously or not, his hopes, his fears, his glimpse of heaven. This factor must remain a recurrent counterpoint to the technical approach to historical analysis that has so far dominated the descriptions in this book. The rational is supported and balanced by the emotional, the practical by the inspired. From this synthesis artistic achievements are derived.

The characteristic features of this period are the form of the arch, which has now become pointed, the tall thin windows, the general accent on height and verticality, and all the structural features arising from this. As already described, the pointed arch and the ribbed vault had been discovered during the Norman period. The first experiments were made somewhere about 1130 and they were to bear full fruit during the next century. Often Norman walls were decorated by a bas-relief pattern of intersecting arches. Although the pointed arch was a structural necessity, not only because it was a means of overcoming the vaulting problems described in the last chapter but because it was far stronger than the round arch and exerted far less lateral thrust, it is by no means impossible that the first idea of a pointed arch was derived from this pattern.

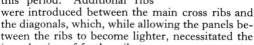

The pointed arch was used exclusively in the vaulting of this period. Additional ribs were introduced between the main cross ribs and the diagonals, which, while allowing the panels between the ribs to become lighter, necessitated the introduction of further ribs along the ridges of the vaults against which the intermediates could lean.

Another interesting feature of the change from Norman to Early English was the increasing use of the chisel instead of the axe for stone carving. Previously carving, though often barbaric in its richness, had been in very low relief, clinging closely to the parent stone. Now considerable undercutting was achieved, and it is fascinating to see how the later 12th-century stone carver loved to bring his designs out in high relief and how he made the formal clinging patterns cut by his predecessors sprout from the stone. In its fully developed Early English form, the decoration of capitals became a deeply undercut very formalized pattern of leaves with a strong feeling of supporting the weight of the arch above, or a deeply grooved pattern of concentric rings of

45

mouldings. These powerfully moulded designs were dramatically appropriate to the ill-lit 13th-century interiors, achieving great strength of contrasting shadow and high-lit stone.

Early Norman—Late Norman

No longer were the simple zig-zags and geometrical shapes used as they had been. The old zig-zag pattern, by increased undercutting, became a series of completely hollowed out pyramids, known as 'dogtooth' ornament.

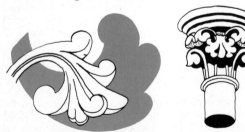

Early English

46

A startling change, too, had come about in window design. Towards the end of the 12th century, glass for windows became available and life had become more settled so that the church was less likely to be used as a place of refuge. This, together with the advantage of the window occurring in the thin wall between the buttresses, enabled the builders to make their windows larger. The typical early window of

the period was tall and thin, with the new pointed arch at its head like a lancet. Soon groups of lancets were arranged together between pairs of buttresses. The desirability of making some sort of hood to prevent driving rain from running down the face of the building into the window was realized, and this gave the builders the idea of coupling the groups of windows together, and

finally of punching holes through the blank spaces left between the hood moulding and the lancets.

This is called Plate Tracery, and in its later stages it was further elaborated into trefoils and quatrefoils. This style of Early English architecture is sometimes called 'Geometric'.

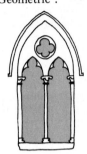

The Norman pillars of the last century were made of rubble with dressed stone faces. Now columns were made with solid blocks and were decorated with completely detached shafts of polished limestone or Purbeck Marble. These shafts were restrained with small bonding stones that make the characteristic 'rings' seen at intervals up their length. In the later stages of this period the shafts were to become merged with the parent column to form a multiple column that further increased the verticality of the design.

The doorways of this period are simpler than their predecessors, and have the pointed arch and not the round. They have the deep parallel mouldings instead of the Norman ornaments and the columns at the sides are detached from the jambs, and are more often in one shaft of stone than were those in Norman work.

Early English builders were very fond of detaching shafts from their background, and it is one of the chief characteristics of their work. This increased desire to have their details free-standing is evidence of an increased interest in space. They were no longer, as the Normans were, so interested in mass, but liked to create a feeling of spaciousness by allowing the eye to travel past objects in the immediate foreground and glimpse possibilities of further spaces beyond.

The castles of the period were much more elaborate than the simple Norman keep. Halls, for a degree of comfort that was impossible in the keep, were built within the walled ring, or, if none existed, walls were built. These were sometimes concentric with the keep or built up to it, the keep then becoming the principal tower in the walls. Crenellation and all the intriguing features of medieval military architecture, like chutes, down which to pour molten lead or boiling pitch, portcullises and drawbridges, all were invented towards the close of the period.

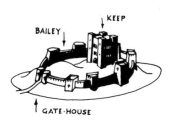

13th Century Castle

CHAPTER 4

The Decorated Period
14TH CENTURY

*

In the 14th century the simplicity and economy of Early English building gave place to a more highly decorated style. No longer were church builders content to make an unadorned pinnacle or spire without decorating it with knobs and crockets of stone; the simple, narrow windows of the preceding century now became a riot of colour and curved tracery. Buildings generally became more profuse in decoration, better lit, and more lavish in their proportions. The accent was all

14th-century Cathedral

on gaiety and elaboration. Glass had by now become far less of a rarity, and the highly decorative coats-of-arms, crests and blazons of the nobility, no less than the greater light-heartedness of the buildings, express the increased prosperity of the country.

Domestic buildings, other than those of a purely military character, had become more common as

TINTERN ABBEY: EARLY 14th CENTURY

the homes of a growing class of reasonably wealthy yeomen. This was also a great period of improvement and enlargement of the parish church. The

Decorated Parish Church

gloomy little churches of the previous century with their narrow windows and shed-like aisles and lack of clerestory lighting, no longer fulfilled the more exacting needs of the people, who wanted light and cheerfulness in their religion as in their lives. The castle was by now as impregnable as it was ever to be, surrounded by high-

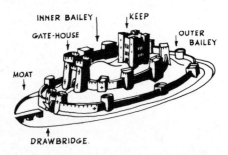

A Late Castle

towered curtain walls. The new plate-armour was succeeding the old chain-mail and military sports such as the tournament were popular. All was gay and colourful, human and brave, just as Chaucer described it.

The second half of the century was overshadowed by the calamity of the Black Death (1348–49), after which very little big building was done. However, a larger measure of independence was gained by the hitherto unpaid labourer class, for labour was in short supply after the plague, a factor which gave the serfs an advantage over their employers. The unrest following on the attempts of the landlords to rectify the inevitable inflationary tendencies that the labour shortage brought about was a contributory cause to the lack of building activity.

Manor-houses became of some importance during this century. Although there are few examples left, and even fewer of those of preceding periods, the development of the house is of considerable importance. The nucleus of the medieval house was the hall, and round this nucleus the house-plan continued to develop until the Renaissance. Houses in early Saxon times were single-unit wooden buildings consisting of a roof supported on wooden posts and walls. In the centre was an open fire, the smoke escaping where it might. The aristocracy had similar but better built

A Saxon House

halls. Round the fire the servants ate and slept, whilst the lord of the house occupied a raised dais at one end. With the Norman conquest the hall idea was not abandoned, the castle keep incorporating a precisely similar hall on the first floor. By the 13th century, conditions had become more secure and the fortified manor-house was a practicable proposition. This was a development of the original Saxon hall, but with

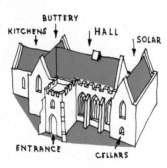

14th-century Manor House

various improvements. Built in stone or brick with a timber roof, the house now consisted of a large room, open to the roof, with the same open fire. This was the hall in which the servants and retainers lived; at one end was the solar, or private room, for the lord of the manor and his family, a room usually on the first floor leading off the raised dais where he had his meals, and at the other end were the kitchens, separated from the hall by screens. The entrance was at the side, at the kitchen end, and beneath the solar was a storeroom. A classic example of this typical arrangement is the hall of the Castle of Stokesay, in Shropshire. By the 14th century further improvements and additions had been made. The manor-house now consisted of the main hall, still open to the roof, divided from the kitchens by a buttery, over which was a guest room. The entrance was elaborated into a porch over which a gallery for musicians was sometimes built. As yet the various elements—the hall, the kitchens, and the solar—are roofed over separately, the solar and buttery or kitchen roofs running at right angles to the main roof of the great hall.

Bricks were used almost for the first time since the days of the Romans. They made their appearance in East Anglia, where contact was closest with the Netherlands, whence the bricks came. Foreign innovation as they were, bricks were used only in secular buildings and in this century only in a few isolated examples. The great flood of popularity for bricks was not to come for a very long time. The normal building material for any wealthy building was still stone, and not for many years were the common people able to build in anything but the most perishable materials. The small domestic buildings that have lasted from this century are those of the rich merchants or well-to-do farmers, people of small account when compared with the great barons, but richer by far than the peasants.

The principal contribution of the 14th century to the ecclesiastical architecture of this country was the development of the window, together with an easily recognizable widening of the shape of the arch. No startling change came over the design of buildings as a whole, no new structural principles were evolved. This is a period of development rather than invention. The increase in availability of glass, together with the new fashion of using imported coloured glass in the windows, assisted the designer to a conception of the window on a scale of size and beauty as yet unknown.

Decorated Cathedral

The early Norman window had sometimes consisted of two openings linked with one arch. In the next century we have seen how the Early English builders continued this idea, by introducing plate tracery by piercing the blank wall enclosed above the openings with simple circular or quatrefoil holes.

In the 14th century this develops into true window tracery, consisting of curved bars of stone all supported on vertical bars or mullions. The

elaboration of small arches and pierced shapes into
trefoils and quatrefoils followed.

From this geometrical basis where steeply

pointed arches and circles are the only motifs
used, the ogee—convex and concave—arch was
evolved.   This is a 14th-century innovation and is
the basis of most curvilinear tracery.   Once freed
from the rigid plain shapes of the so-called geometrical tracery,
the masons lavi-
shed their skill on
a riot of curved
stonework, em-
ploying free, fan-
tastic shapes of
great beauty.
This was partic-
ularly so in the
early part of the
century.

The method of
allotting centuries
to architectural
periods must not
be taken too liter-
ally.   They are the
centuries during

57

which the bulk of the typical work of the periods was carried out, but many country districts were

years behind the times and many a great religious house was half a century ahead. Thus in 1340 the choir at Gloucester was being built in the Perpendicular style, well ahead of its time, while in remote districts, particularly where there was a strong local building tradition, the Early English methods were still in force.

Early English vaulting developed in the Decorated Period only in its greater technical efficiency. The panels between the ribs were made lighter and the number of ribs was further increased, forming star-like geometrical patterns. The many rib-junctions were decorated with stone knobs or bosses, elaborately carved with faces, grotesques and foliage. The fine stylish carving of the 13th century developed into naturalism and an over-elaborate technique, with a consequent loss of fitness of form. The same decadence in design is noticeable in the capitals of columns, where the foliage no longer has the feeling of simple strength and the supporting quality of Early English work.

Columns are taller and still more slender than those of the Early English period, better built, but with no free-standing shafts. The shafts have now become joined to the parent body of the column to make a cluster of piers, while the mouldings round arches and in capitals are far less deeply cut and a general flattening out of detail and design is noticeable. The startling contrasts that were necessary in the gloom of Early English buildings had become redundant and over-accentuated in the better-lit interiors of the 14th century.

14 TH CENTURY

13 TH CENTURY

Castles of this date are comparatively rare, but many older castles were enlarged and elaborated. The military role of the castle was fast declining and the nobles were building huge vaulted halls within their towered baileys, elaborate suites of stone rooms on a scale impossible to confine within the narrow limits of a fortress keep. The castle extends outwards in a complicated series of inner and outer wards, courtyards and rings of walls, towered and embattled. One is tempted to surmise that the technique of military engineering had already far outrun its uses, a state of affairs that was more marked in the next century, when castles were erected for effect and show, indeed almost for fun.

CHAPTER 5

The Perpendicular Period
15TH CENTURY

*

Perpendicular design is unlike any other, is very easily recognizable, and is wholly English.

Its keynote is that of sophisticated restraint, coupled with a mechanical precision of detailing and proportion that seems to lend to the masonry a quality almost metallic. Walls are finished so

finely as to seem infinitely thin, while the windows are so large that the building is more like a huge glass box held up by fine shafts of stone than one of stone walls with windows pierced in them.

We have seen how during the preceding centuries the efficiency of building methods has steadily improved, growing from the crude beginnings to a great degree of technical perfection. We have seen also how from the aesthetic standpoint stone carving and the general elaboration of form have degenerated, and how the too-skilful mason has allowed his chisel to run away with him.

What is to be expected next? Clearly, either a further elaboration of what was tending already to become over-elaborate or something entirely new.

Up to this time all the building styles in England had had their counterparts on the Continent, particularly in France. It is now, at this last stage of Gothic building, that English builders strike out for the first time on a line of their own. In France the last stages of Gothic developed into a style known as Flamboyant, all curves and carving. But in England a return to comparative simplicity and austerity of design took place. Why this should have been is not certain.

Perpendicular Cathedral

It has been said that the shortage of craftsmen due to the Black Death made for simplification in design. This, even if it be true, can only be a small part of the solution. Some of the earlier works were designed and built in the Perpendicular manner before the Black Death, and after the epidemic was over hardly any building was undertaken for some time. After the enforced pause, the new style emerges practically in its only and fully fledged form.

One immediate effect of the Black Death was the growth of the change in the farms from arable to pasturage for sheep, as a measure for saving labour. The wool trade was soon booming and a tremendous increase in trade, marketing and transport took place. Bridges and town halls, market places and inns were by now being built in great numbers. Yeoman farmers made their fortunes, and many men who had been tied to the land as virtual slaves were now building their own manor-houses. Great numbers of parish churches

15th-century
Market Cross

were built and additions to many cathedrals were carried out with the money made from wool.

Perpendicular Parish Church

The art of printing (1477) aided the stimulus that had been given to the founding of colleges and schools, many of which were built during this period.

Owing to the introduction of gunpowder, castles were no longer able to withstand sieges. Consequently castles as such were no longer built,

KING'S COLLEGE CHAPEL, CAMBRIDGE: LATE
15th CENTURY

and the more settled condition of the country towards the end of the century under Henry VII provided an opportunity for building many houses designed as non-defensive homes. Such magnificent places as Bodiam, Hurstmonceaux, and Warwick were among the last of the genuine castles built for defensive purposes. But even these were built very largely for show.

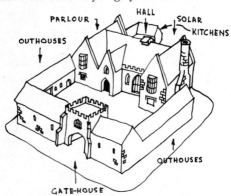

15th-century Manor-House

In spite of all the fundamental social changes that had been taking place, progress was still, by modern standards, astonishingly slow. Nevertheless, the manor-house continued to develop. Extra accommodation for guests and servants—for travel was at last becoming an easier matter—was provided by building extra suites of rooms and outbuildings in the form of a courtyard in front of the entrance door of the hall. The hall was still used as before, the open fireplace still sending its

64

smoke up to the open beams of the roof. The importance of the dais at the end of the hall was often accentuated by a larger window that reached to the floor. Big windows of this nature had to face into the courtyard, which was defended by a gate house, for although in the long term the country was becoming more secure, the times were troubled still. Oriel or bay windows were often used in the solar and more important upper-floor rooms, such as that over the buttery. The solar was now provided with a fireplace, and the walls of the upper chambers were even panelled in oak.

As regards the detailed appearance of Perpendicular buildings, the most noticeable distinguishing features are the lower and flatter arch, which appears in most work, the simplification of window tracery, which is universal, and the beautiful development of rib-vaulting into its last and most highly advanced stage, fan vaulting, which is seen only in the most expensive work of the period.

As a means of spanning over a space with the smallest rise in height, the four-centred arch was evolved. This and its variations, although not universally adopted, are very frequently found in Perpendicular work.

In church building the natural development of the structure continued, resulting in larger windows filling the entire wall space between even deeper buttresses.

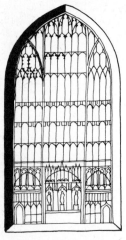

The large windows had to be subdivided by stone members to keep the glass in place, and a simple grid of vertical and horizontal stone bars was evolved. The windows were so large that unconnected vertical mullions would have been too long for stability. Where the main arch springs, the bars branch out into simple tracery, the perpendicular members of the grid usually being continued through the pattern to the underside of the arch itself. It is from this characteristic that the style of building derives its name. This method divided the windows into similar rectangular shapes and each panel could be made to contain a separate picture of a story or separate saint in a series, in stained glass. It is a satisfactory and dignified solution to the problem of window design on a vast scale.

The well-dressed stones that the

masons were able to cut in this period gave the walls a clean, bare appearance that contrasts beautifully with the elaboration of the windows. Frequently in the more expensive buildings these wall surfaces were decorated both within and with-

out with a delicate relief pattern, a repetition of the motifs that made up the tracery of the windows, making of the whole wall a modular pattern into which the windows fit as an integral part, rising to the culmination of perpendicular architecture, the roof.

Roofs in both stone and timber had by this time developed considerably. In late work, stone vaults were brought to a great pitch of refinement in which the fan-like springing of many ribs assumed the form of an inverted curved cone, like a trumpet standing on its mouthpiece. The ribs curved up and out to the semi-circular top of the cone that rested against those of the neighbouring cones, forming between them a series of almost flat diamond-shaped panels in the ceiling. The original diagonal ribs lost their importance and

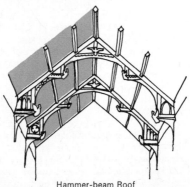

many intermediate ribs, all of the same thickness, were introduced.

The vault ceased now to be a pointed tunnel intersected by other similar pointed tunnels and became a curved shell of great complexity.

The calculations necessary to cut the stones for such a vault so that each fitted exactly into place are a measure of the skill of the 15th-century craftsmen.

The vault-ribs formed panels, patterned to echo the window tracery, and were so close together that now rib and panel could be cut from one piece of stone. The ribs, acting as mere stiffeners to a shell, could now be quite freely arranged.

For centuries the roofs of halls and smaller

Hammer-beam Roof

churches had been built in timber. It is in the Perpendicular period, however, that timber roofs become most highly developed. They are of all types, from the simple tie-beam roof to the elaborate double-tiered hammer-beam roof. It is the hammer-beam roof that takes pride of place; for splendour it has no equal. The great roof of Westminster Hall is the chief feature of the whole building, a fact that was evidently clearly realized by the designers, who kept the rest of the building extremely plain and simple in order to form the better contrast. The art of roof making was particularly highly developed in East Anglia, many Norfolk churches having splendid roofs quite out of proportion to their size and importance.

In following the tendency towards simplicity, and a preference for rectangular shapes, the 15th-century designer made the hood moulds over his doorways square, filling in the triangular space between the hood mould and the arch with simple cusping or other plain patterns, occasionally incorporating a coat-of-arms but never indulging in naturalistic foliage or realistic scenes. Flamboyance is wholly lacking in this type of design. It is all much more restrained, much less exuberant. Pillars were frequently made up of several

shafts that were merged together to such an extent as virtually to become mere mouldings on one shaft, mouldings that recall in their shallow curves and angles the folds of pleated cloth. The capitals and bases tended towards straight-sided polygons, and the abolition of curves here is a noticeable feature.

Mouldings round arches tend to become rather thin, flat and mean, having none of the deep cut or voluptuous quality of the Early English. Carving, where it occurs, is of a highly formalized nature. A complete change has come about from the naturalism of the preceding century. Foliage is made to conform to a set geometrical design, and is frequently so stylized as to be hardly recognizable.

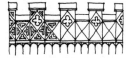

Mock battlements are a very usual feature of this style of building. They are used over and over again, variously decorated, in almost all possible positions. The parapet-walls round roofs and towers are almost always embattled, but in a light-hearted way, the intention to decorate rather than to defend being clear. The liking for battle-

ments went so far that they were frequently used in miniature as decorations to horizontal members of window tracery, carved screens, tombs, and so on, in either stone or wood as the occasion demanded. This form of decoration was popular possibly because it fitted so well with the prevalent custom of using rectangular panels as the basis for so much of the decoration. The parapets would frequently be carved with quatrefoils, lozenges, and circles, executed in bas-relief or inlaid with some contrasting material as split flint on stonework or dressed stone on brickwork, according to the local materials of which the building was made.

During the course of the century many university colleges were founded, and this is an indication of the trends of thought of the time. Learning was rapidly becoming less the exclusive property of the Church. Even in England, the Renaissance was afoot.

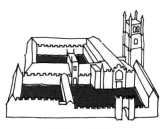

A University College

*

PART TWO

BUILDINGS OF THE
TRANSITIONAL PERIOD

*

CHAPTER 6

Renaissance
1500–1625

*

The Renaissance was a rebirth of Greek and Roman ideas that supplanted medieval ways and thought. Its influence invaded every sphere of life, and caused a fundamental change in the appearance and planning of European buildings. The movement originated in Italy early in the 15th century, but its effects on the architecture of England did not become apparent until a century later. The Italian renaissance owed its inspiration to the works of the Romans, and Roman culture was based to a great extent on the civilization of Ancient Greece. It is, therefore, in Greece that the story of Renaissance building really begins.

The large stones that could be cut from the Greek marble quarries had allowed the Ancient Greeks to use huge beams rather than arches. They preferred beams because they were more in keeping with their traditional timber construction, and were more satisfying aesthetically. Through

---

ST. PAUL'S, COVENT GARDEN, BY INIGO JONES 1631

centuries of trial and error the Greeks had evolved proportions for the various parts of their buildings designed exactly to satisfy their very highly developed aesthetic sensibilities. By the fifth century B.C. they had developed this beam-and-pillar building type to its final form, the most perfect example of their work being the Parthenon at Athens.

Greek Temple

The columns that the Greeks used were of three different sorts, varying with the different localities. Each sort of column had its own special proportions, mouldings, decorations, and so on, and the entire unit of construction and decoration is known as an Order. The three Orders are Doric, Ionic, and Corinthian.

Later the Romans colonized Greece. Being less concerned with aesthetic refinements but needing to build very much larger structures than could possibly be roofed over by the largest beam, the Romans adopted the arch as the structural basis of their buildings. However, they were so impressed by the superior culture and refinement of the Greeks, that they took their beam-and-pillar building elements and incorporated them into arch-and-dome constructed buildings, often merely as applied decoration.

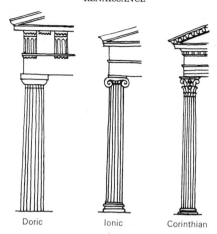

Doric   Ionic   Corinthian

When the Romans adopted these elements they abandoned the more delicate refinements. Substantially, however, the Orders and general proportions remained the same. The ordinary details of Roman buildings were the semi-circular arch, the pediment, or Greek gable-end that they had adopted, and the three Orders now used decoratively,

Roman Arch

often superimposed one on top of another in the various stages of a multi-storey building.

By the 13th century the great buildings of the ancient peoples were in ruins, skeletons of a forgotten past,

The Pantheon, Rome

75

used only as quarries for ready-made building material. But Italian writers of this date were already rediscovering the classical poets and philosophers, and were formulating a new conception of life on classical lines of reason and objective enquiry. The ever-present problem of reconciling medieval principles with man's growing knowledge of life as he saw and experienced it was gradually becoming more and more acute as his knowledge of ascertainable physical facts increased. As time went on men turned to the classics for a solution of this fundamental problem, and a full realization of the heights of civilization that had been reached by the ancients without the aid of any such medieval principles gave rise to grave doubts of their truth. By thought along these lines they prepared the ground for a revolt against the medieval outlook of mysticism and religious preoccupation.

Centuries later in far-off Constantinople an Easternized classical tradition was still strong. The old libraries of Constantine were still stocked with the works of the older civilizations. When in 1453 this city was sacked by the Turks, Western Europe, and particularly Italy, was flooded with refugees. Among them were many learned scholars who had escaped with a wealth of antique manuscripts and treasures from the libraries. It needed but this extra incentive to consolidate in a people already ripe for change an enthusiasm for classical culture. This was already becoming a ruling passion with influential Italians, who, by their patronage of the arts, enabled the splendid Italian architects, artists, and craftsmen of that time to execute many works in which they clearly expressed their enthusiasm for antiquity and the classical materialist outlook. Roman buildings were studied and surveyed, the ruins were reconstructed, grandiose Roman planning was admired and copied, and antique building forms became fashionable in the same way that classical processes of thought were becoming universal. The new Italian buildings, however, were very different from the Roman buildings, for they fulfilled quite different purposes. But, being inspired by the enthusiasm for classical culture as interpreted by the 15th-century Italians, they always included some classical motifs such as the pediment, the dome, semi-circular arches, or straight beams, the Roman mouldings and the Roman columns.

Italian Chapel

On their journey from Italy to this country the new building forms suffered many changes. They came via France and the Netherlands, and were even further debased by the English builders,

Italian Villa

who did not understand them, misapplied most of them, and were unaware of the exact proportions that the Greeks had worked out so long ago.

The initial stage of muddle and experiment that resulted did not last for more than a hundred years. Inigo Jones, who had studied the exact rules of classical proportion that had been formulated and tabulated by the Italian architect Andrea Palladio, was the first English-

77

man to build according to the correct rules. By the time of Jones's death in 1652, the period of transition from medieval to classic building was at an end.

Ionic   Debased Ionic

The transition has been divided for convenience into two main parts, Tudor, which is largely medieval in detail but owes its *raison d'être* to the Renaissance movement, and Elizabethan and Jacobean, which is classic in detail, although at first very inaccurate in application and proportion. Although Elizabeth was a Tudor, the architectural character of her reign falls more conveniently into the second category, and is indeed wholly different from the first.

During the medieval era we have learned to expect the structural problem to govern all and every part of the building. Now, in the 16th, 17th and 18th centuries, this basic consideration no longer so obviously applies, because the problems the builders had to solve were very much simpler. They seldom had to attempt such feats of engineering as the medieval church and cathedral builders, for not only were the majority of their buildings on the domestic scale, but they were not concerned to make them as light and dynamic as possible. To build in a 'good Roman manner' was their aim, and the Romans relied on an appearance of great solidity to achieve their effects of magnificence. No longer were the lateral thrusts set up by arches and vaults of paramount importance except in the few really large buildings employing domes and arches. The lateral pressure of all but the largest arch could easily be absorbed in the more solid masonry allowed by the new aesthetic.

Building forms no longer bore the close and obvious relationship to structural necessity that they did in medieval times, for they were forms arising from a long and involved history of change in which many had lost their original purpose, becoming applied decoration. Their admiration for the ancients gave the Renaissance builders the desire to adopt these features, and their rapidly increasing scientific knowledge gave them the structural ability to do so.

Here we enter an age in which spiritual attainment is of secondary importance, intellectual ability paramount. It is a highly civilized age of great artificiality.

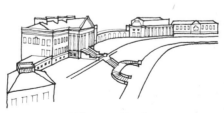

18th-century Mansion

CHAPTER 7

Tudor

1485–1560

*

Tudor buildings are wholly Gothic in form, but they are nearly all secular. This is scarcely surprising when the unpopularity into which the Church had fallen is considered, together with the fact that there were by this time plenty of churches for everyone. The dissolution of the monasteries provided large tracts of exploitable land on which farms were started by neighbouring gentry, who also built smaller farms and cottages for their tenants. At the same time Henry VIII was instituting a spending programme—financed by the confiscated church properties and the prosperous wool trade—and was encouraging the building of large country houses and palaces to increase English prestige abroad.

Consequently, although the architectural character of this period is very much like the last, the accent is on domestic rather than ecclesiastical building, and so the scale is much more intimate. Windows and doors become smaller, buildings become more complicated, chimneys and fireplaces become common. The most characteristic feature of Tudor buildings, however, is the use of *brick*. This building material had suddenly acquired an almost universal popularity that spread from East Anglia. Some bricks were shipped across to this country from the Lowlands as ballast in the returning wool ships, and some were made in East Anglia by Belgian and Dutch brickmakers, who had set up yards there. Cardinal Wolsey and Henry VIII both used brick for their palaces, and countless smaller houses and cottages were built of this new material.

Tudor Palace

The typical Tudor Great House presented a delightfully romantic appearance. Built in warm red brick, its most noticeable feature was the gate-house. This often consisted of a broad low arch, flanked on either hand by tall octagonal towers, crowned with mock fortifications. Steep roofs and fantastic brick chimneys like cork-

screws, many gables and turrets, provided a variegated skyline. Above the door a coat-of-arms carved in brick or stone proclaimed the nobility of the owner, for many families at this time had only recently risen to wealth and power and thus ostentatiously displayed their new-found social status.

Castles were by this time quite unnecessary, and any fortified buildings of this period were just so

ST JAMES'S PALACE: EARLY 16th CENTURY

much stage scenery to provide what their owners considered a suitable background for their position and wealth.

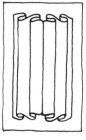

A Linen-Fold Panel

The interiors of Tudor mansions are usually panelled from the floor almost to the ceiling with narrow panels each made of one plank of oak, which are either plain or are carved in the characteristic pattern known as linen-fold. The fireplace is a huge open affair with a flattened arch over it, and in the houses of the wealthy there is usually a coat-of-arms or some other decorative feature carved in stone, wood, or brick as an overmantel. The chimney-stack was introduced at this period largely because of the new fuel—coal. This was found to produce an intolerable smoke. Wood smoke previously was allowed to get out of the house through the roof, or in the larger halls—in castles and the like—a large open fireplace with a rudimentary flue leading obliquely through an outside wall was usual. Now, however, the necessity for taking the smoke right away

above the house served a useful purpose, for the builders discovered that the fireplace need no longer occupy an outside wall, and that, with a flue taken up vertically from the hall, the great high room, open to the rafters, could now be floored in half-way up, so doubling the available floor space. The new floor was usually left bare underneath, showing between the beams on which it rested, without a plaster ceiling.

The windows are small, their size being governed by the domestic scale and the most convenient size for making an opening casement in iron and glass. They are simple and of a characteristic proportion, and are either single or grouped in pairs or threes with a stone or brick hood over them. They have flat arched heads, cut, more often than not, from one piece of stone, and the triangular spaces in the corners are nearly always cut out in little three-cornered depressions that may be regarded as the last faint remnants of tracery. These windows were normally built of stone let into the brickwork. Larger windows were of the perpendicular sort, with tracery and stained glass as before. The oriel window was much used, and became somewhat larger and more elaborate.

Tudor arches are invariably either four-centered or a modification of the four-centered arch, which is flatter and has straight sloping members rather than curved ones.

As yet nothing has been said of timber buildings, and it would not be correct to leave the impression that all Tudor work is in brick.

In timber districts such as Lancashire, Cheshire and Warwickshire, oak-framed houses were the rule, the details of windows and doors being carved in wood as though they were stone, that is, with little wooden arches and mouldings. A strong oak skeleton was set up and in between the timber members were built light panels of either brick or plaster, according to what local material was available. Often the brickwork in these panels was laid in decorative patterns, either in herring-bone or vertically. This could be done because the bricks were not used structurally but purely as an infilling to keep out the weather. In Tudor work the timbers were always placed very close together with little room for the infilling between. As yet the builders were uncertain of their material, not daring to build the more widely spaced and economical frames that were later adopted. Very often the lower storey was built in brick or stone, with the top storey and roof in timber. The combination of various materials is one of the most delightful features of the Tudor small house.

A Tudor House

In districts where bricks were scarce or where plaster was easily made the famous black-and-white type of building resulted; black beams with whitewashed plaster panels in between. The upper floors of these houses frequently projected beyond the ground floors, giving them their characteristic overhang. This was particularly the case in towns where ground space was limited. Often houses were built of many storeys, each storey projecting beyond the one below till houses on either side of the street practically touched. This practice was discontinued in Jacobean times.

In stone districts the local material was again used to the exclusion of brick, and such alterations in style as were necessitated by a different material are apparent. In country districts where there is a strong conservative building tradition details are seldom a true guide to date. Smaller buildings were still completely Gothic in character for years after the Renaissance, and the detailed history of a locality must be studied before allotting a building to a specific historical period. It is to this fact that the popular misconception with regard to the date of small houses is due. Comparatively few cottages are more than three hundred and fifty years old.

Before leaving the Tudor period mention must

be made of one of the most remarkable buildings in England—Henry VII's chapel at Westminster. This was erected after his death and was executed in the most lavish manner possible. All the features are essentially perpendicular in form, but with none of the restraint noticeable in the earlier work. Here every part of the building is carved and decorated in a labyrinthine multitude of panels. The pinnacle has given place to a most characteristic Tudor motif, the stone, dome-shaped, pepperpot-like top to the buttresses. From the roof stalac-tites of wrought stone seemingly hang—in reality the larger pendants actually support the vaulting—but the elaboration of carved work and the complication of the structural principles used so obscure the under-lying meaning of the roof that the real magnificence of the engineering feat that the Tudor masons achieved is  not apparent. The roof was designed in this elaborate manner in order to make the fashionable flat-headed window extend right up to the under-side of the vault. The chapel is a marvellous work of craftsmanship and ingenuity and, although it does not necessarily represent the highest achieve-ment of Gothic art, it is the Gothic building carried to its last stage. Development from here could clearly go no further. A dead end had been reached. By this time the Renaissance move-ment in Italy was already some hundred years old, and occasionally Italian craftsmen accepted com-missions for works of art for wealthy or royal foreign patrons. In later years, during the time of the religious persecutions under Elizabeth and

Mary, this practice was largely discontinued, or at best only possible for artists upholding the faith of the reigning sovereign of the time. In this case, however, the Italian craftsman Pietro Torrigiano was commissioned to execute the tomb of Henry VII, which forms the centre-piece of the chapel and is the earliest well-known example of Renaissance work in the country.

The contrast between the simple humanity of the cherubs that sit at the corners of the tomb and the encrusted magnificence of the medieval structure that surrounds them is a remarkable example of the essentially different standpoints of the Gothic and Renaissance designers.

CHAPTER 8

Elizabethan and Jacobean
1560–1620

*

After the death of Henry VIII less building was undertaken, for the king's spendthrift policy had left the country practically bankrupt. However, at the accession of Elizabeth the religious turmoil was largely quelled, and the prosperity of the country began to revive. The wool trade was not so prosperous as it had been, and the Queen wisely encouraged the farmers to increase their arable land as a change from sheep farming. This necessitated the employment of far more labour on the farms, and an increase in small houses and cottages resulted. The new policy succeeded well enough and the country again enjoyed a considerable measure of prosperity. Wealth was now distributed among a very much larger class of reasonably well-to-do people rather than con-

Elizabethan
Small House

centrated into a few hands, a fact that further augmented the boom in small house building. Considerable big building in the form of new country mansions also took place, and many older houses were altered and modernized. Hospitality was considered of prime importance and the new aristocracy used to vie with one another, and half ruin themselves, in their attempts to make their homes the most fitting resting-places for the queen on her royal visits. The tremendous popularity of the sovereign was part of a great

upsurge of patriotic feeling at least partly brought about by the successful defeat of the attempted Spanish invasion.

Elizabethan Cottages

Great houses began now to be tricked out in all the fashionable details of what passed in Elizabethan England for Italian Renaissance. The Italian craftsmen attracted to the court of Henry VIII were giving place to Protestant Lowlanders, for the Catholics had thought it wiser to withdraw. The great trade that had been carried on with the Netherlands made this association a natural one,

Elizabethan Mansion

THE TOMB OF THE POOLE FAMILY, SAPPERTON, GLOS: EARLY 17th CENTURY and printed illustrated books of architectural details from these countries were much used by English builders.

The development of the large houses continued from the manors of the Tudor period. The chief features of the Elizabethan great house were an effect of symmetry in the façade, a long gallery, an imposing staircase, and a formal garden incorporating such features as yew walks, terraces, and fountains. The symmetrical layout is the first indication of a change towards the classical plan.

The country had for some time been peaceful enough for the enclosed courtyard to be dispensed with, the gate-house, if built at all, being only for display. The layout had thus gradually assumed an E-shape, the vertical stroke representing the main hall, the two long horizontals the sides of the old courtyard—now incorporated into the kitchens

The E Plan

on the one hand and the old living-rooms on the other—and the short horizontal being the entrance porch, moved to the centre for the sake of symmetry. The 'hall' became a large imposing entrance hall and was less and less used for living in, while the staircase that usually led from the hall was of the open-well rectangular sort, often with an elaborately carved balustrade and newel posts. The long gallery—obscure in origin and purpose—was placed on the first floor, and was a feature that the wealthy man of the time seemed reluctant to do without. The fundamental change that had come about here was that the hall and the living-rooms had changed places in their relative importance. The hall had become relatively unimportant, whereas such rooms as the long gallery had become the chief features of the house. Usually built in stone, for with the Renaissance movement brick was losing popularity for important buildings, with curved Dutch gables or else with a straight, balustraded parapet and a wealth of classical detail, the Elizabethan mansion is nothing if not imposing. Chimneys were usually grouped in pairs or threes, were often made

to resemble classic columns, and were usually rectangular instead of the fantastic corkscrew shapes of the preceding period. Windows are larger than ever before, consisting of a simple grid of vertical mullions and horizontal transoms with diamond-shaped or square leaded panes between. The windows have no arches but are completely rectangular, and are topped either with a Gothic dripstone or with a classical moulding.

It is by the mixture of Gothic

ideas, like the hood mould over a window, with classical detail such as columns, broken pediments, and so forth, that Elizabethan work is most easily distinguished. It is always the necessary functional details of a building that cling longest in the older idiom, for whereas the craftsman is willing to try his hand at a new thing provided that should it prove unsatisfactory no disastrous consequences will follow, he is most reluctant to attempt to change from his traditional way of, for instance, keeping the rain out of a window. So in the embellishment of fireplaces and all internal fittings we see the earliest changes towards the new fashions, and in the deep-rooted basic structural idea of the house the Gothic tradition lingers longest.

The architectural expression of the Renaissance movement in England was as yet only in the form of fashionable decoration. No fundamental change had been made in planning except for a tendency towards symmetry. It was not till Inigo Jones came home from Italy that the Italian style began to influence the basic shape of buildings.

The front doors to the houses of the wealthy expressed in their elaboration the prevailing spirit of hospitality and ostentation. This feature was made the most elaborate part of the house. Almost invariably it had a round semi-circular arch flanked by classic columns of dubious parentage and was often surmounted by a fantastic pile of carved stonework, incorporating the arms of the owner, statues of classical heroes, pinnacles, and all manner of carved work.

The smaller homes continued in the Tudor tradition and adopted the Renaissance decorative motifs much more slowly. Fireplaces and chimney-stacks now became common, and a larger staircase than the previous rude, ladder-like affair was incorporated. Otherwise the plan remained very much the same as it was before, with the central hall now floored in half-way up, flanked on either hand by the living-quarters and the kitchens. Timber buildings were more efficiently and economically constructed, the timbers now being spaced more widely apart.

In Jacobean times, when for reasons of safety from fire the king decreed that the overhanging houses that were such a characteristic feature of towns should no longer be built in London, the practice of building the frame in one single piece from ground to eaves became general.

The most characteristic detail of Elizabethan and Jacobean work is the use of strap ornament. This, used lavishly both externally and internally on almost all features, is of Germanic origin, and

usually takes the form of a bas-relief geometrical pattern of interlacing straps that is unmistakable. Sometimes the motif was applied in fretwork to a balustrade, sometimes classical foliage is flavoured with a strap-like quality, and nearly always the pattern is sugared with a liberal sprinkling of lozenges, ovals, and diamonds, like jewels in a fancy-dress crown.

Columns often have a strange growth of decoration that climbs like ivy up a tree-trunk to as much as a third of their height. With regard to the details of the interiors, the walls of rooms were nearly always panelled in oak or decorated with panels of moulded plaster. These were often in patterns based on the round-arch form, or in later work were plain but for classical cornice mouldings round the top. Imported coloured  marbles were much in vogue for decorative fireplaces, and black and white marble was imported to make chessboard floors to the halls of the wealthy. Ornament had run completely wild—fat classical columns and Gothic heraldry being inextricably mixed with cupids and strap ornament.

In Jacobean times the character of the work becomes a degree more classical but a great deal more Teutonic in flavour. The strap ornament gives way to a formalized foliage, and heavy-busted female caryatids are all too frequently employed on columns that are larger at the top than at the bottom.

Decorative plaster ceilings were much in fashion in the Elizabethan mansion. Most of the patterns were derived from late Gothic fan vaulting, and pendants in miniature imitation of those in the roof of Henry VII's chapel at Westminster were used as a decoration, hanging like stumpy stalactites from the intersections of the plaster ribs.

As the 17th century progressed, so the quality of the decorative work became more correct. By the time Inigo Jones died much of the more gross and vulgar features of Stuart detailing had given place to a sober but ponderous classicism.

A HOUSE IN DEDHAM, ESSEX: EARLY
18th CENTURY

PART THREE

BUILDINGS OF THE
CLASSICAL ERA
1620–1800

*

CHAPTER 9

Inigo Jones and Christopher Wren
1620–1720

*

It is during this period that individual architects became of importance. Buildings were planned, not by members or organizations such as the Church in which their names became lost, but by independent architects or architects holding a post under the Crown. Architecture now became dependent more on mind and intellect than on craftsmanship and material.

At the beginning of the century there was little accurate knowledge of classical proportions or usage. No one had made a sufficiently careful study of ancient buildings, or of the laws that Palladio had evolved from them, to build anything that was not a very debased and second-hand version of classic proportion.

Sir Christopher
Wren

Inigo Jones was the first man to bring the pure Italian Renaissance style to this country. He was an architect who had studied in Italy for some years, and was appointed as Surveyor-General to the Crown in 1615. The style he built in was pure Italian with as few modifications as possible. His buildings were very un-English in character, with

Queen's House, Greenwich

the severe flat line of the parapet which hid the roof, and the solemn, regularly spaced columns along the front. His two most revolutionary designs were the Banqueting Hall in Whitehall and the Queen's House in Greenwich. The latter was of great importance, for nothing had been seen like it in England before, not only in its strict classical details but in its general shape. The plan and conception of this house profoundly influenced all subsequent domestic design. It was completely rectangular, having no gables or other projections; it was completely symmetrical, and it had the principal rooms on the first floor. This last was an Italian fashion, lending added height and magnificence to the building. The rooms on the first floor were very high and grand, with large windows, and the layout gives great scope for magnificence in the staircase.

Inigo Jones' influence was to be profound, for men like Christopher Wren and all those who followed him owed their basic conception of classic design to his pioneer work.

The problem that now arose was how to adapt this new foreign building technique to English ways and English climate, English materials and English craftsmen. To Inigo Jones this problem was of secondary importance. Several country houses were designed and altered by him, or at

A House after Inigo Jones

least owe their form to his immediate influence. Here the steep roofs and the vast chimneys sit somewhat awkwardly over the classic façade. As yet the Italian and the native idioms are at variance. Such English features as steeply pitched roofs, chimney-stacks, large windows, and all the parts of a building that owe their character to a cold, dull, damp climate had to be fitted to the new style. Could this problem be resolved whilst still retaining the richness, dignity, and repose that are the results of true classical proportion? Christopher Wren was the man who, to a great extent, achieved the solution.

This immensely versatile man was a mathematician, an astronomer, and, above all, an inventor. It is to his enquiring inventiveness that so much of his success is due. He used traditional

English building materials, brick and ordinary roofing-tiles, inventing new ways of using these in order to keep within the limits of classic rules. He also popularized the use of Portland stone in London.

Brick and Stone Combined

He, like Inigo Jones, was appointed Surveyor-General to the Crown when he was about thirty years old, and started almost immediately on the immense task of rebuilding the churches of London, burnt down in the Great Fire of 1666.

The house remains the predominant building type of the 17th and 18th centuries, and next in importance after the house comes a great quantity of public and commercial building, such as customs-houses, hospitals, pump-rooms, market-places, shops, and so on. The church building of London was mostly accidental because of the Fire, although, of course, some churches were built to meet the needs of the growing suburbs.

A Customs House

By the end of the 17th century, services in the reformed Protestant Church were very different

A Hospital

affairs from the old medieval ones. Gone was the sense of mystery, gone the barrier between the priest and the congregation. The new conception of a church was a large room in which as many people as possible could hear the preacher in comfort, a room that was full of light and clarity and common sense. Wren's interiors are clean, beautiful rooms, with gold-and-white plaster work and large pale windows; with galleries round the walls for the extra people that lived in a crowded city. The altar was often in the body of the church rather than at the east end. It is a building fit for a service in which the importance of the spoken word— the sermon—is paramount, rather than one in which may be held the mystic ritual of the older faith. The point is exemplified by the prominence now given to the pulpit in these churches.

A Market Place

Outside, these buildings are nearly always very simple, and are usually crowned by spires or towers that rise above the roof tops of London and mark the parishes. It is by these spires that Wren's churches are chiefly known. They are tall piles of beautifully proportioned stone and are very ingenious, for classical motifs are here welded into what is after all essentially a Gothic shape, and they show in their structure the greatest engineering cunning.

But apart from his churches, as has already been said, Wren influenced the design of houses, both in town and country, and it was under his influence that, at the beginning of the 18th century, the characteristic Queen Anne house evolved.

A Queen Anne House

A City Spire

To fit the classical way of building to the ordinary well-to-do gentleman's home, that is, to build a house that was not a palace but still retained all the simple dignity of a classical design, was the problem solved for the first time in the Queen Anne house.

In this type of design gables were undesirable, and hipped roofs were used instead, a roof that sloped up from the eaves to the ridge from all four sides, thus preserving the horizontal eaves line all round the building. The eaves line was treated like a cornice, with the small curly brackets in imitation of the

A Queen Anne Town House

carved ends of rafters that are found on ancient Roman buildings. If the number of floors that a certain house needed meant that the house would look too high for its width, that is, too high a shape to conform with the laws of proportion that the design demanded, the top floor was put above the eaves in the roof, the windows projecting through in the form of dormers, leaving the heavy horizontal line of the eaves or cornice uninterrupted at the lower level. This device was used by Inigo Jones and his pupil, Webb, but without Wren's delicacy and homeliness of proportion.

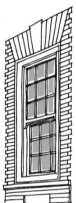

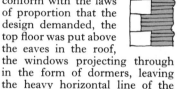

These houses, following the Queen's House at Greenwich, were nearly always of a simple rectangular shape, and were to all outward appearances completely symmetrical. Their angles were frequently treated with quoins, or corner stones, or with blocks of brickwork, alternately long and short, projecting slightly from the surface of the wall.

Their windows had heavy wood or stone frames, thick glazing bars, and the same long

105

and short patterns on a smaller scale worked up the sides in a slightly raised or darker brick. At their head, a stone or raised brick keystone was often introduced, and their flat arches were occasionally decorated with a 'cupid's bow' type of scroll.

The feature which has influenced our urban landscapes more than any other is undoubtedly the sash window, introduced early in the 18th century. It is to be seen in many Queen Anne houses, became almost universal in the Georgian period, and remained the standard domestic window until the end of the 19th century. This ingenious mechanism shows clearly the new

scientific approach of the contemporary designers. Queen Anne doorways were almost invariably given canopies, supported on characteristic brackets. These doorways were usually made of wood or stone, but in town houses were sometimes built up in fine brickwork. In this case a pediment would usually be supported on half-columns instead of a canopy on brackets.

Inside the houses of the wealthy, the ceilings, if decorated, had heavy plaster garlands of fruit, flowers, and vegetables running round them in ponderous geometrical patterns. Carving of this sort was 'in the round', almost standing free from its background, and all the fruit, dead partridges, potatoes, and so on that were incorporated were treated with the utmost realism.

Grinling Gibbons is today the best-known exponent of this type of carving, usually in wood. The character of the rooms was dignified and solid, the walls panelled in large deep panels, the ceiling in heavy solemn patterns.

The 17th century was one in which architectural character made considerable changes, but in different degrees at different levels. The poor man's house had hardly changed at all, but was slowly becoming less medieval in its details and was built of more permanent materials. It remained, however, essentially the same as it had been in the past. On the other hand,  the rich man's house had changed completely from the higgledy-piggledy layout of the last century, with battlements and turrets, oriel windows, and clipped yew hedges, to the symmetrical, steep hip-roofed mansion, ponderously chimneyed, with its square windows framed like pictures and its solemn tall rooms. Again, churches had conformed to the requirements of a new form of religion, and were clothed in all the frills of the new building technique, a change that is perhaps more startling than that of the house, since the evolution was more spasmodic.

In the next century we shall see the further development and refinement of these tendencies, the growth of the town house and of town planning, and the beginning of the industrial revolution.

THE CROSS BATHS AND BATH STREET, BATH:
LATE 18th CENTURY

CHAPTER 10

The Eighteenth Century
1720–1800

*

Eighteenth-century building is characterized by
its great refinement. It is the architecture of a
highly civilized age. The predominating building
type that flavours the whole century is the Town
House. This, the Georgian terrace house, was
built in very great numbers and was to a high

18th-Century Houses

degree standardized. The general acceptance of
one standard was possible because one philosophy
was believed, a philosophy of materialism and of
reason. It was a somewhat circumscribed and
brittle philosophy in which there was little room
for half-tones. A thing was either right or wrong.
This applied to all activities, and in the sphere of
architecture it implied that there was only one
right way to build. This was the standard; to
depart from it would be bad taste—almost bad
manners. The house, although the principal
type, was far from being the only sort of building.
The 18th century is one packed with incident,
and great numbers of all classes of buildings,

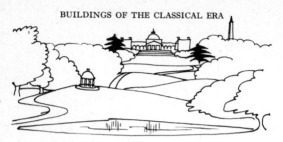

The Avenue

including shops, public works, coaching inns and commercial buildings, were erected.

The wealth of the country was once more concentrated into fewer hands. The rich were becoming prodigiously wealthy, and owned huge tracts of land, often as much as half a county, which they enclosed rigidly. Common land became scarce, and consequently the livelihood of the smallholder became more precarious. The only way of life left to him was either to work as a labourer for the big landowner or to seek employment elsewhere. The towns, which were centres of growing commerce, absorbed many of these smallholders and a depopulation of the countryside gradually began.

Within his enclosed land the wealthy man laid aside enormous areas as private parks in which to keep ornamental deer and trees and in which to build his house. So powerful were these men that they were able to remove a whole village and build it elsewhere if it were in the way of their grandiose schemes. They laid out their parks with wonderful avenues of huge trees many miles long and often hundreds of yards broad, down which could be seen vistas of rolling grass, cunningly punctuated with artificial lakes and delicate sophisticated classical monuments—little temples, bridges, wells, or grottoes—and so contrived as to terminate in some outstanding local feature, such as a church tower or a hill. If no such feature existed, one would be built—a triumphal arch, an imitation ruin, a mausoleum, or an obelisk. For such men no flight of fancy was too extravagant, but it was extravagance on the grand scale: no tawdry spendthrift whim of the moment, but an extravagance on a long-term policy. None of the great landscape artists of this time can ever have seen his schemes as he meant them to be seen, for none of the splendid avenues would have reached anything approaching maturity when he died. Life in the 18th century must have seemed wonderfully secure for such plans to have been conceived and carried out, for a private fortune spent willingly on posterity argues a remarkable faith in the future.

A Mausoleum

In the early part of the century these great houses were often designed in the Baroque manner, employing classical motifs freely to produce an effect of grandeur, without regard for the strict rules of proportion.

The Baroque, as a term applied especially to an architectural type rather than to a form of decoration as is its more general sense, implies a style that owes little to convention and all to effect. The designer allows his imagination to run riot, and produces splendid compositions in stone and brick. The Baroque is immensely three-dimensional, producing in the onlooker a strong consciousness of the mass of the building and of the space enclosed within it.

Sir John Vanbrugh and Nicholas Hawksmoor were the chief exponents of Baroque in England. Although great size is by no means an essential quality of this style of building, in Vanbrugh's hands it became titanic.

In his palaces, Cyclopean columns overshadow great mountains of masonry, so solid as to take the breath away. Blenheim Palace is his greatest work; Castle Howard and Seton Delaval are also among his well-known great houses. They rely for their effect of magnificence not on a profusion of rich and fussy details, but on their

Blenheim Palace

broad massing and heroic proportions. Few mortals could hope to live up to such Olympian homes. Hawksmoor is best known for his London churches which follow in the Wren tradition.

The 17th- and 18th-century gentleman delighted to immortalize himself in lavish tombs and many may be seen in the contemporary classic Baroque manner, contrasting strangely with the sober Gothic churches in which they are situated.

After Wren, Vanbrugh, and Hawksmoor had died, the spirit of experiment and invention died too. Architecture settled down to a conventional good taste, and Palladian features such as doors, windows and mouldings may be seen in buildings of almost any date from the middle of the 17th century onwards.

A Palladian Doorway

Large houses, although they continued to be laid out with considerable extravagance, became in themselves less generous, more cold and aloof; they have an air of aristocratic superiority quite at variance with the bombast of the Baroque.

Meanwhile, what of the less fabulously wealthy? Prosperous towns as trading centres, like Norwich and Bristol, or as fashionable resorts, such as Bath, were growing rapidly. London itself was expanding at a great pace. Towards the end of the 17th century the density of houses in towns had given rise to the invention of the

A Georgian Terrace

terrace as a means of preserving dignity suitable to the wealth of the occupant together with economy in space. By building a whole street of houses all run together and treated as an architectural whole, comparatively small houses could be given all the dignity of a palace. Thus we see in London, first in the Temple and other Inns of Court, built before the end of the 17th century, later in proper houses, the first terraces; the first of what was to become in the 18th century the general method employed for a vast residential urban development.

Usually the houses were four storeys high, with a short flight of steps up to the front door. Below the ground floor there was a basement, the principal rooms being on the first floor.

The standard details of such houses are a familiar sight in almost any town. The sash window was almost the only window employed in all but the remote country districts until the middle of the 19th century. Tall and dignified, with delicate wooden glazing bars, glazed in standard-sized panes of glass, the Georgian window does much to harmonize whole districts of our towns. The front doors are generous and are delicately panelled, with semi-circular fanlights over them. Inside the front door, a rectangular or oval stone staircase leads up, balustraded in fine wrought-iron.

The 18th-century builders laid out their terraces in simple straight streets, fine big squares, with gardens in the middle, in crescents and circuses, one opening out of the next, forming vistas and avenues of masonry and brickwork terminating in clumps of trees that are the square gardens, just as in the country they laid out avenues of trees, terminating in buildings. The insistence on vistas and avenues, which is a natural outcome of a symmetrical layout, was a technique that the Renaissance architects had taken from ancient Rome, and was a complete innovation to England. This fine planning was not for the nobility or the very wealthy; it was for a large and growing upper middle-class.

Town planning of this sort would not have been possible if every man had built his own house. The original owner of the land—and huge tracts were in the possession of single land-owners—if he thought it profitable, would 'develop' it as a speculation, laying it out as attractively as possible to captivate the

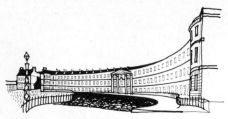

An 18th-Century Crescent

wealthy tenants who would pay him a suitable rent. Sometimes these men would employ a contractor to carry out their own schemes; sometimes the contractor or architect would plan the whole layout as a private speculation of his own. Four architects, the two Woods and the two Dances, both fathers and sons, were responsible for developing large areas of Bath and Dublin respectively, while later in the century the brothers Adam did much to develop still more of Georgian London, and developed a style quite their own. By this time the design of terrace houses was to so standard a plan that it is

only in the general layout and the details that one style changes from the next. Most of the Adams' work was in town housing, and some of the terraces they laid out are among the most delightful in the country. They refined all the features of the Georgian town house, taking as the inspiration for their designs the details of ancient Greece or Pompeii.

116

Adam doorways had beautiful spider's-web fanlights over them, the glazing bars made in cast lead; windows were taller and with thinner glazing bars than ever before. Balconies were made of fine wrought or cast iron. Everywhere the Greek honeysuckle pattern was used, in plasterwork on the columns, which were now often made quite attached to the

main building and of a flat rectangular section, in the iron work of the balconies, in ceilings, and in the decorations over the fine marble chimney-pieces.

The artisan and working classes were housed in precisely the same style of building as the wealthier middle class, but on a much reduced scale. Neat little terraces of two-storey houses or neat little brick box-like cottages are a familiar sight in our towns and villages.

Georgian Shop Window

A further aspect of the Georgian street scene that is still a feature of many provincial towns is the large number of beautiful shopfronts. Arched, bowed, barrel-shaped, or plain, often still with their elegant lettering in gold on black, they lend us a tantalizing glimpse of a more spacious and more leisured age.

*

PART FOUR

BUILDINGS OF THE INDUSTRIAL ERA 1800 TO THE PRESENT DAY

*

CHAPTER 11

The Nineteenth Century

*

The 19th century is one of violent change and the history of its architecture is extremely complex. We can do no more than give a very generalized account of architectural development.

The architecture of the century falls into three categories: Regency architecture, Revival architecture and what, for want of a better term, we shall call Industrial architecture. The first belongs to the first thirty years of the century and is a direct continuation of the Georgian tradition. The second overlaps the first in time and is a movement for reviving various past *styles*, for erecting buildings in the *manner* of past ages. The third runs as an undertone to the other two throughout the 19th century and continues into the 20th. In this category fall such buildings as the Crystal Palace, the iron and glass railway stations and the great bridges of Telford, Brunel, Baker and others, and, although many of Blake's

---

THE BRIDGE AT IRON BRIDGE, SALOP, 1779
THE FIRST LARGE BRIDGE TO BE BUILT

'Dark Satanic Mills' were erected in the 18th century, they too are included in this chapter for convenience.

During the Regency and the reign of George IV, middle-class homes continued in the classical tradition. The domestic architecture of this period belongs in character to the preceding century. It is so refined and civilized that it

Regency Villa

recalls the golden age of culture rather than the smoke and turmoil of the Industrial Revolution.

The typical Regency house is built of brick and is

A Nash Terrace

often covered in stucco or painted plaster. The buildings have a delicate Graeco–Italian flavour lent them by their refined proportions and painted wall surfaces. The fashion for stucco was imported from Italy and was originally colourwashed to imitate stone. The shining paintwork we now admire is a comparatively recent innovation, but it does

120

permit us to appreciate the material for its own sake rather than as a substitute.

Under the influence of archaeological researches  by Lord Elgin, Byron, and other amateur antiquaries, an enthusiasm for Greek and Graeco–Egyptian motifs had grown up, a tendency already fore-shadowed in the Greek motifs employed by the Adam brothers. All the richness and refinements of Greek carving, fluted columns and the delicate folds of classical drapery was reproduced in elegant stucco, and elegance is the essence of Regency architecture.

The grander buildings like the Nash Terraces around Regents Park, continued to be planned in the grand Roman manner, but were tricked out in all the refinements of the contemporary version of classical Greece.

The smaller and less osten-tatious terraces and houses of the Regency, also often in stucco, are simply a less robust version of the Georgian. Almost any town with preten-sions to fashion has a number of such buildings with their refined glazing bars, gossamer-fine iron balconies roofed in curving metal like Chinese pagodas, or curved bay windows, bay fronts and round-topped front doors. Wall surfaces were nearly always plain and roofs were often of a low pitch with wide projecting eaves, recalling the warm Mediterranean, an effect that was deliberately heightened by the use of painted wooden shutters.

For some time past a romantic movement had been afoot that found beauty in rusticity, a whimsical return to medievalism and other exotic building forms. This had at first shown itself in artificial Gothic ruins in the grounds of great landowners, carefully designed *cottages ornées* for

Brighton Pavilion

their tenants and such fashionable curiosities incorporated in their classical mansions as a Gothic library or a Chinese dining room. This, to our eyes absurd but often charming fashion, reached its apotheosis in the Brighton Pavilion, a riot of oriental fantasy.

But in the centres of industry and in the poor quarters of the towns, the social evils resulting from the increase in population and commerce were becoming all too evident. Grace, peace and dignity seemed no longer to exist in a world of ugliness, meanness and squalor. Thousands of new houses were built in towns whose boundaries could often not be expanded outwards owing to the system of land tenure still existing. The resultant ill-built insanitary slums constituted an environment as horrible as any yet devised.

Men of sensibility felt this state of affairs keenly, but instead of fighting the evil, they attempted to escape it. They attempted to put the clock back, to return to what they thought of as the more genuine ways of the middle ages, to create for themselves a dream world divorced as far as possible from the unpleasant realities they deplored and the artificial classicism they despised.

A School

Their reaction also took the form of an admiration of the handcrafts, for at that early stage of industrialization machine-made articles were patently inferior to those made by hand. The handcraft movement started by Ruskin and William Morris has been a powerful influence in education ever since.

However it is not to be supposed that architects were seriously attempting to recreate a genuine medieval environment. In their search for a new aesthetic approach, they used medieval *styles* and *forms*, in buildings otherwise suited to contempor-

Greek Revival

ary needs, to express their admiration for medieval methods and principles. The search for a fresh approach is a recurrent theme throughout the 19th century and is typified by, among others, the Pre-Raphaelite Movement, the Aesthetic Movement and the self declared Art Nouveau itself.

But the medievalists did not hold the field undisputed. Much domestic building, more particularly the large estates in the fashionable suburbs, continued to be built in the classical manner, faced with painted stucco, the details becoming coarser and more heavy handed as the century progressed. Many commercial, civic and public buildings besides were erected, offices, town halls, libraries, museums and the like, in classical style.

We are thus presented with the unique spectacle of two basic *styles* of building concurrently in vogue. The so-called 'battle of the styles' was conducted on the broad basis of classical versus medieval. This was an academic polemic regarding opposed philosophies, as much as an argument about building styles as such.

The architect was now for the first time in history exercising his skill in two separate ways; firstly in de-

Commercial Classic

124

signing buildings fitted to their purpose in a functional way, good hospital plans, noble law courts and so on; and secondly, and seemingly quite separately, deciding in what style they should be built. It is from this unique approach to architectural practice, which lasted for little more than a century,

Gothic Revival Church

that the all too common misapprehension arose regarding the role of the architect as essentially that of 'beautifying', a view held even today by a surprisingly large number of otherwise well-informed persons.

By the latter half of the century, the number of styles available for choice appeared almost unlimited and ran the gamut of European cultures down the ages from Romanesque, through Venetian Gothic to Tudor, Italian, French and Dutch Renaissance and many others besides.

A turn towards simplicity gave rise to the Aesthetic Movement of the Seventies. This took the architectural form of a liking for red brick, red roof tiles, painted woodwork and simpler interiors favouring dark oak and blue Delft china. The simplified 'Queen Anne' of Bedford Park and the Dutch gables of Kensington and Chelsea epitomize the movement.

The Art Nouveau was another movement, this time towards a more sophisticated and elegant simplicity with its well-known decorative motifs based on organic plant forms. The restrained and disciplined work of Charles Rennie Mackintosh and his colleagues, which typifies its architectural expression in this country, contrasts vividly with the elaborate, decadent, *fin de siècle* atmosphere of the style on the Continent where it originated.

But these were essentially philosophically and aesthetically based movements. From the beginning of the century the supposed incompatibility of industrial necessity and aesthetics had left the needs of industry and transport to be met largely without the help of architects. Engineers came into prominence as apart from architects; their works, ironically enough, are amongst the greatest contributions to 19th-century architecture.

The engineers in particular welcomed such new materials as science made available. Sheet glass and cast iron (later steel) were the two most important new materials that had arrived in quantity by the middle of the century. The huge glasshouses built at this time, the best known perhaps being Decimus Burton's Palm House at Kew, were the inspiration, and to an extent the prototypes of Paxton's Crystal Palace, a vast

Crystal Palace

prefabricated building made of standard sheets of glass and standard girders of iron.

The railway companies were not slow to see the possibilities of such a structure applied to a railway terminus, a building into which whole trains could steam and which could have a roof so high up that the smoke from the engines would hardly affect it. They enclosed in these shells of iron and glass enormous volumes of space, creating single-cell buildings far larger than anything that had been built before.

Market halls with iron and glass roofs were also built. In all these iron buildings the decorative possibilities of cast iron were not ignored and many have beautifully enriched structural members, recalling the structural embellishments of the Medieval era.

The Forth Bridge

Canal and railway bridges of great size were constructed of iron and steel. The Forth Bridge, completed in 1890, takes its place as one of the really great bridges of the world. It is over $2\frac{1}{2}$ kilometres long and in a single span reaches half a kilometre. There was little of decadence or *fin de siècle* about the work of the engineers.

We referred at the beginning of this chapter to Blake's 'Dark Satanic Mills'. The mills and warehouses erected during the latter part of the 18th century and the early part of the 19th are to be admired today not only as part of our industrial archaeological heritage, but for their functional architectural qualities.

They are nearly always built as purely functional buildings of brick or stone, without any decoration whatever except perhaps for a louvred bell-cupola on the roof or a pedimented entrance doorway. Yet these buildings are almost invariably satisfactory to look at. It is not only their ample proportions, solid construction and noble size that appeals to us, but their evident fitness for the purpose they were to fulfil; in this lies the germ of the functionalist ideal that had such a far-reaching influence on the Modern Movement. It is the successful choice of materials, proportions and forms that raises these simple practical buildings from the sphere of efficient engineering to that of good architecture.

The 19th century is one of great contrasts. Pomp and splendour contrasts with appalling squalor on the one hand, and on the other a welter of imitation and fancy-dress building contrasts with splendid feats of engineering.

Miners' Cottages

CHAPTER 12

The Twentieth Century

*

By the beginning of the 20th century the pressures of commercial expansion, together with the growth of population and wealth, conspired to force the pace of development in the field of architecture as in all else.

The larger and more elaborate buildings demanded by these influences were made possible by advances in technology, the more important being the development of steel and concrete for structures and the introduction of electricity.

These factors produced profound changes in the shape and size of new buildings. The new structural materials allowed large spans and slender supports and thus a freedom in planning hitherto unknown. The introduction of cheap electricity, by making possible fast passenger lifts and good safe artificial lighting, enabled buildings to be designed that were far taller and deeper in plan than had been possible before. Close collaboration between architect and engineer had become a necessity for the successful design of such buildings. The ever quickening pace of social change too was creating the need for massive housing programmes and slum clearances. The building industry, responding as ever to economic pressure, was relying more and more on factory-made materials, for craftsmen's time was no longer cheap and machines were becoming efficient.

All this was hardly a scene in which the individualistic and romantically inclined Victorian architect, with his traditional pre-occupation about building styles, could find a place. Individualism, romanticism and building styles were

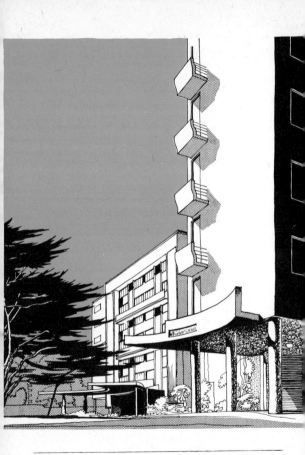

FLATS AT HIGHGATE, LONDON:
20th CENTURY

all as irrelevant at the turn of the 20th century as a leaning towards the picturesque had been in the 19th.

The history of the Modern Movement, for such is the name given to the re-appraisal of architecture which was necessary in the 1900s, is rooted in the 19th century. We have seen how the need to simplify contemporary design had inspired the various break-away movements, starting with the traditionally motivated Arts and Crafts Movement in the mid-century and finishing with the almost complete freedom of the imaginative Art Nouveau at its end.

The urge towards simplicity, however, showed itself in this country for the most part in domestic architecture, exemplified by the work of Charles Voysey in the 1890s, following the early work of Norman Shaw. Still within a traditional framework, he eliminated almost all period flavour and invented what amounted to a new aesthetic of quasi-rural domesticity, featuring horizontally arranged rows of windows, white walls and huge chimneys. He, and later Sir Edwin Lutyens, demonstrated for the first time that houses for the comparatively wealthy need be neither elaborate nor pompous. This was nice simple building suited to its purpose, but still using traditional materials in a traditional way. The step towards

Charles Voysey

using the new materials and techniques already made available by industry had yet to be taken; that this step was not taken is probably because houses, by their scale and nature, require for their construction no more demanding techniques than those that had been in common use for centuries.

During this period, the Garden Estate, Garden City and Garden Suburb ideas were conceived. The slums of the industrial revolution had been allowed to 'happen', and few had done more than deplore the result. Towards the close of the 19th century some wealthy and enlightened employers laid out housing estates for their work-people, with gardens for the houses, space for allotments and planted or grassed verges to the roads. Port Sunlight and Bournville were products of the 80s and 90s and were followed by the Garden Cities and Suburbs of Letchworth, Welwyn and Hampstead.

These developments in English domestic architecture were not without their effect on the Continent and in America. Communications between all parts of the world had by the turn of the century become so rapid and universal that international styles became inevitable; national differences in aesthetic and technique had almost ceased to exist, except in so far as these are conditioned by different climates.

But national temperament still governed the speed with which new ideas were accepted, so it is that in Holland, Germany and France more rapid change was possible than in conservative Britain. It is in these countries, more particularly in Germany, that the Modern Movement developed.

Meanwhile, during the first half of this century in Britain most buildings continued in period style, simplified as a concession to escalating labour costs perhaps, but essentially Classical, Baroque, etc., while domestic architecture reverted to a polite but emasculated Georgian. However, in less self-conscious buildings, particularly those designed for popular amusement and recreation such as the cinemas, restaurants and exhibition halls of the inter-war years, a new style emerged, owing little to functionalism but expressing in new materials its acceptance of the hectic age of speed, electricity and jazz. This popular style was known as 'Moderne', and its decorative forms as 'Art Deco'. These forms are as well known as those of the Art Nouveau, designs based on a combination of streamlining and triangles, in the form of zig-zags, sunbursts and general angularity. Like the Art Nouveau before, it had no obviously direct influence on the Modern Movement, which indeed was already advanced in its development, for during the early part of the century on the Continent important new contributions to the philosophy of architectural design were being made.

In Germany, first in small groups and later nationally, the modern approach to architectural design came to be accepted. By the 1920s the most celebrated of the pioneering groups had been established, the *Bauhaus* in Dessau. Once again, as in Georgian England and as in the Arts and Crafts Movement, the idea behind the *Bauhaus* teaching was that design should be all-embracing; unity of approach in all the arts was essential. These pioneers admired the great engineering achievements of the 19th century. They and others like them believed that design should spring from first principles and owe nothing to past styles or past techniques. The most readily available materials, the products of a highly industrialized society, should be used in the most practical and functional way; the purpose for which the building was to be used and its structural needs must be permitted to dictate its form down to the last detail. Used with sensitivity, these radical functionalist principles should produce good architecture. Certainly they produced a new architecture, startling in its uncompromising severity. However, the economy, the honesty, the common sense, above all the clarity of expression of the

Frank Lloyd Wright

new architecture all appealed to a generation that had seen too much of the traditionally inspired and over-elaborate styles of the preceding years. The movement was taking place moreover in an age that was caught up in the post-war social revolution and that was ripe for new ideas.

Le Corbusier

By the 1930s the Modern Movement was well established on the Continent, but in England its expression was spasmodic and for the most part confined to buildings commissioned by enlightened private individuals rather than by public bodies. Its acceptance in Britain today as the norm for any new building is surely the outcome of the economic and social climate that has developed since the Second World War.

After the Second World War there was a huge back-log of building to be made up, aggravated by the physical destruction of the war itself. The back-log was the spur needed for the development in Britain of modern architecture. A rational and functional approach to design had now become an economic necessity, simultaneously with the emergence of a whole generation of modern architects who had trained in progressive schools during the 30s, who had absorbed the philosophy of the *Bauhaus* and who were inspired by architects such as Frank Lloyd Wright and Le Corbusier, the two great exponents and propagandists of modern architecture and the outstanding architectural geniuses of the inter-war years.

Modern buildings owe their rectilinear shapes

to modern structural techniques; steel and concrete lend themselves to slab, post and beam construction. Arches and roof trusses are no longer necessary, so windows and doors are rectangular and roofs flat. The large spans and cantilevers or overhangs made possible by steel and concrete have not only freed the interior of the building from the large piers necessary in medieval and classical buildings, but have also made

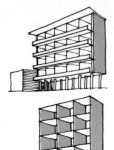

A Concrete Building

possible the elimination of the external wall as a structural element, so that the wall can be in front of or behind the supporting columns; it can be made entirely of glass or other light material and may assume the function purely of a weatherproof envelope of variable shape independent of the structure.

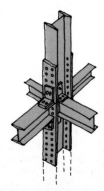

We have stated previously that buildings owe their form to the purpose they are to fulfil, to the materials available and to the skill of their builders. This rule holds good today as it has always done, for today these factors are very different from what they were a hundred years ago, and of course modern buildings are totally different too.

Firstly the purpose they are to fulfil depends upon the needs of society. With the coming of the welfare state and all the social changes of today the emphasis is on comfort for the many rather than luxury for the few, and this influences the design of workplaces as much as it does that of homes and places of entertainment. Domestic service is virtually a thing of the past and a very high proportion of the population owns its own private transport. Different sorts of buildings are needed, such as air terminals, research laboratories and computer centres; the needs of more familiar building types such as hospitals or factories are vastly more complicated than they used to be, while some sorts of buildings such as power stations or office blocks are of a different order of magnitude from their predecessors.

Secondly transport and modern industrial techniques have made available for the builder a much increased variety of materials. Machine-made materials, whose behaviour under working stress can be precisely calculated, are available; economy of means demands the extensive use of machine-made materials in a machine age and inevitably a high degree of standardization results. In this category, too, falls the technique of pre-fabrication; wall panels complete with glazed windows, indeed whole service-core elements

including bathrooms all ready equipped, can be made in the factory and lifted into position in the building.

Thirdly the skill of the builders has changed from the craft-guild approach to the modern factory-based production line for a wide range of building materials, from steel joists to wall-boards and plywoods. Except in a few trades, fashioning and putting the material together on site has become less a matter of high individual craftsmanship and more one of control by experienced management of team-labour. Programming and scheduling such work has become a vital skill in all large modern building projects. But the skill of the builder, in the wider sense when speaking of it as a prime factor in shaping architecture, goes much further than these considerations and embraces the total skills available to the community, including all the multifarious activities of the industry from the production of raw materials, via the design of the machines which shape them, to the skills of the engineers and architects who direct the work.

It would be absurd to describe in greater detail the appearance of the various elements of modern buildings in the same way as has been done in earlier chapters for the historic building styles. In this chapter and to some extent in the chapter on the 19th century, we have been describing ideas and events more than buildings. Change is brought about by ideas and events and those which gave rise to the Modern Movement are of the greatest importance. They provided the motivation for a break with the past in architectural terms that is more significant and complete than any other in our history. We tend to take what we see for granted; it is not until we pause to think that we realize how total, sudden and unprecedented this change has been.

As yet, modern architecture may appear austere and uncompromising, brutal or dull. This is because the new building techniques have only recently grown out of their infancy. If austerity, like beauty, may be said to be in the eye of the beholder, it is surely much exaggerated therein by a century and a half of conditioning in rich Victorian and Edwardian romanticism. Austerity is not a fundamental characteristic of modern architecture. The economic use of machine-made materials and of contemporary scientific structural methods are, however, essential results of our social structure and are no passing phase.

We hope that we have made the point that modern architecture is not just a 'style' in the sense of a decorative technique that can be applied to a building. It is the outcome of a philosophy of design which finds its roots in the social and technological revolution which western civilization is experiencing. Modern architecture is the organization, form, structure, and technology not only of buildings in isolation but groups of buildings, the spaces between, the neighbourhood, the town—in fact the artificial environment of mankind.

VISUAL INDEX

Norman

Norman Church (*p. 27*)

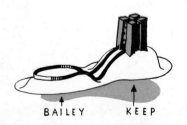

Norman Castle (*p. 26*)

Norman

See p. 27

141

Early English

Early English Cathedral (*p. 40*)

Early English Parish Church (*p. 40*)

Early English

See p. 44

Decorated

Decorated Cathedral (*p. 56*)

Decorated Parish Church (*p. 52*)

Decorated

See p. 55

Perpendicular

Perpendicular Cathedral (*p. 61*)

Perpendicular Parish Church (*p. 63*)

Perpendicular

See p. 65

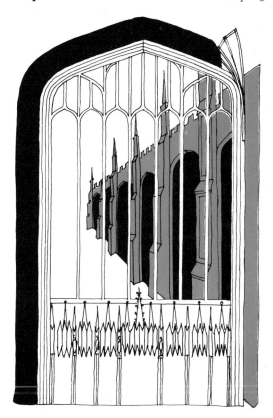

Tudor

Tudor Palace (*p. 81*)

Tudor House (*p. 86*)

Tudor

See p. 81

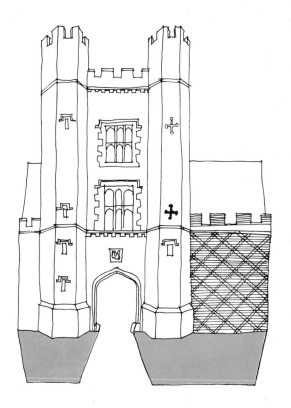

Elizabethan and Jacobean

Elizabethan Mansion (*p. 91*)

Elizabethan Cottages (*p. 91*)

Elizabethan and Jacobean

See p. 93

Classical

Queen's House, Greenwich (*p. 100*)

A House after Inigo Jones (*p. 101*)

Classical

See p. 100

Baroque and Queen Anne

Queen Anne House (*p. 104*)

Brick and Stone Combined (*p. 102*)

A Public Building

Baroque and Queen Anne

See p. 112

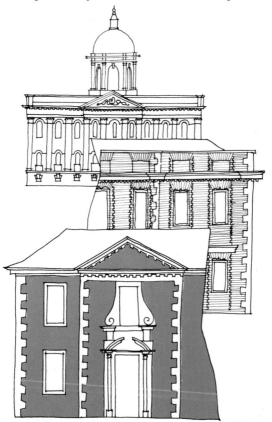

Georgian

Georgian Terrace (*p. 114*)

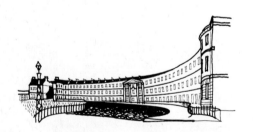

18th-Century Crescent (*p. 116*)

Georgian *See p. 114*

Regency

A Nash Terrace (*p. 120*)

Regency Villa (*p. 120*)

Regency *See p. 120*

Norman

See p. 35

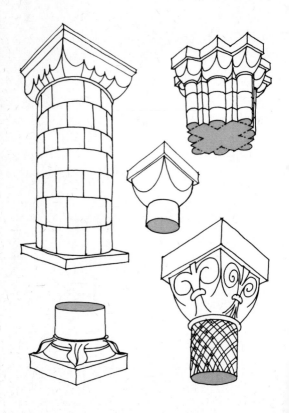

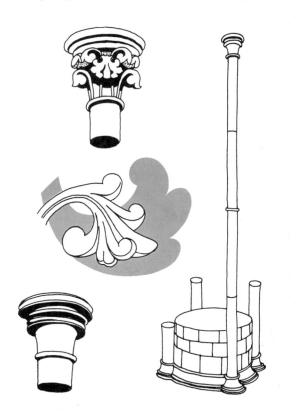

Perpendicular

See p. 69

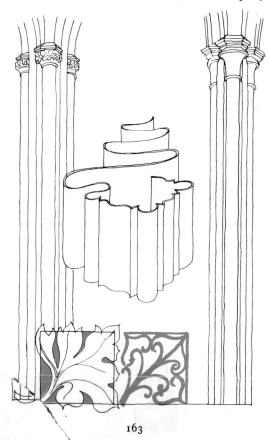

Elizabethan and Jacobean

See p. 96

Classical

See p. 75

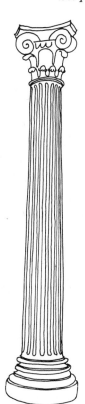

Norman and Early English

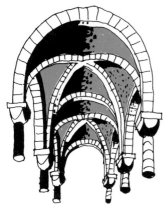

Norman
12th Century
(*see p. 32*)

Early English
13th Century
(*see p. 45*)

167

Decorated *See p. 58*

Geometrical
Patterns

Many Ribs

Perpendicular and Tudor

See p. 67

Elizabethan

See p. 97

Classical and Georgian

See p. 106

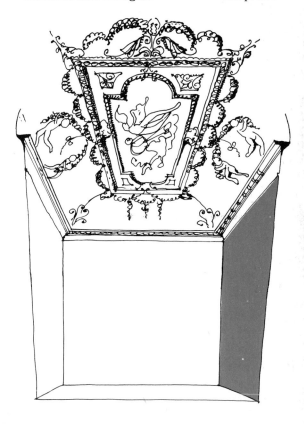

Adam *See p. 117*

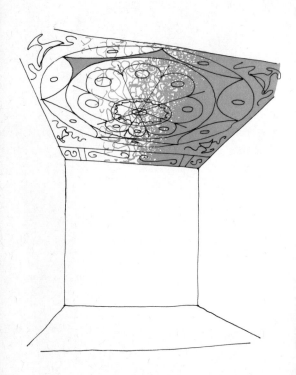

Norman and Early English

Norman
12th Century
(*see p. 34*)

Early English
13th Century
(*see p. 48*)

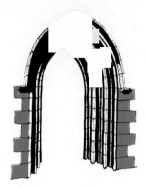

Decorated
14th Century
(*see p. 58*)

Perpendicular
15th Century
(*see p. 69*)

Elizabethan and Jacobean

See p. 95

Classical *See p. 113*

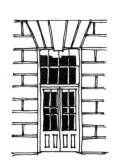

Queen Anne

See p. 106

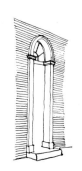

Norman   *See pp. 34 and 35*

Early English

See p. 47

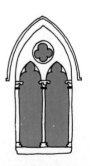

Decorated

See p. 56

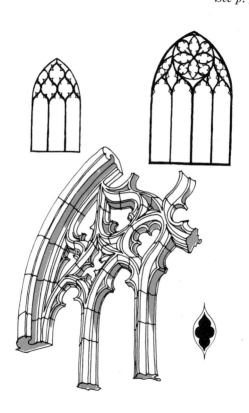

Perpendicular

See pp. 65 and 66

Tudor

See p. 84

Elizabethan *See p. 93*

Classical   *See pp. 105 and 113*

Baroque and Queen Anne   *See p. 105*

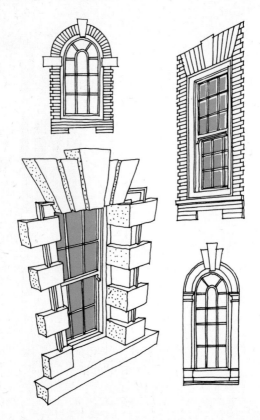

Georgian

See p. 115

Adam and Regency

See pp. 117 and 121

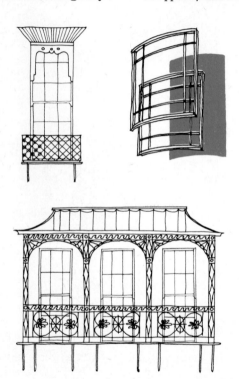

NOTES

CLASSICAL, GREEK DORIC

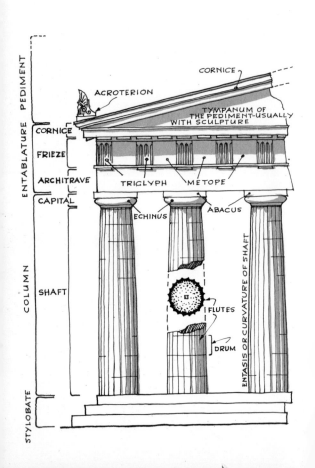

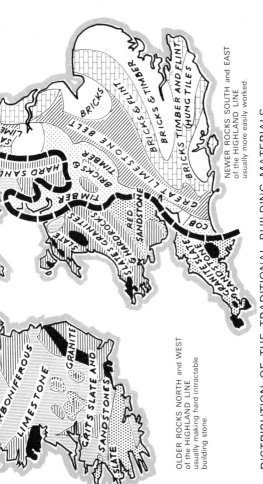

OLDER ROCKS NORTH and WEST
of the HIGHLAND LINE
usually making hard intractable
building stone.

NEWER ROCKS SOUTH and EAST
of the HIGHLAND LINE
usually more easily worked.

DISTRIBUTION OF THE TRADITIONAL BUILDING MATERIALS

The Observer's Pocket Series

ARCHITECTURE

The Observer Books

A POCKET REFERENCE SERIES COVERING A
WIDE RANGE OF SUBJECTS

Natural History
BIRDS
BIRDS' EGGS
BUTTERFLIES
LARGER MOTHS
COMMON INSECTS
WILD ANIMALS
ZOO ANIMALS
WILD FLOWERS
GARDEN FLOWERS
FLOWERING TREES
    AND SHRUBS
HOUSE PLANTS
CACTI
TREES
GRASSES
COMMON FUNGI
LICHENS
POND LIFE
FRESHWATER FISHES
SEA FISHES
SEA AND SEASHORE
GEOLOGY
ASTRONOMY
WEATHER
CATS
DOGS
HORSES AND PONIES

Transport
AIRCRAFT
AUTOMOBILES
COMMERCIAL VEHICLES
SHIPS
MANNED SPACEFLIGHT
UNMANNED SPACEFLIGHT
BRITISH STEAM
    LOCOMOTIVES

The Arts etc.
ARCHITECTURE
CATHEDRALS
CHURCHES
HERALDRY
FLAGS
PAINTING
MODERN ART
SCULPTURE
FURNITURE
POTTERY AND PORCELAIN
MUSIC
POSTAGE STAMPS
BRITISH AWARDS AND
    MEDALS

Sport
ASSOCIATION FOOTBALL
CRICKET

Cities
LONDON